CAMPFIRE GIRLS IN THE ALLEGHENY MOUNTAINS

STELLA M. FRANCIS

Campfire Girls in the Allegheny Mountains

CHAPTER I

THE GRAND COUNCIL FIRE

"Wo-he-lo for aye,

Wo-he-lo for aye,

Wo-he-lo, Wo-he-lo, Wo-he-lo for aye!

Wo-he-lo for work,

Wo-he-lo for health,

Wo-he-lo, Wo-he-lo, Wo-he-lo for love."

Two hundred and thirty-nine girl voices chanted the Wo-he-lo Cheer with weird impressiveness. The scene alone would have been impressive enough, but Camp Fire Girls are not satisfied with that kind of "enough." Once their imagination is stimulated with the almost limitless possibilities of the craft, they are not easily pleased with anything but a finished product.

The occasion was the last Grand Council Fire of Hiawatha Institute for Camp Fire Girls located in the Allegheny city of Westmoreland. The classroom work had been rushed a day ahead, examinations were made almost perfunctory, and for them also the clock had been turned twenty-four hours forward. The curriculum was finished, and the day just closed had been devoted to preparation for a Grand Council wind-up for the fifteen Fires of the Institute, which would "break ranks" on the following day and scatter in all directions for home and the Christmas holidays.

And there was literal truth in this "break ranks" method of dismissing school at the Institute. Since the United States entered the European war on the side of the anti-frightfulness allies, Hiawatha had become something of a military school. The girls actually drilled with guns, and they would shoot those guns with all the grim fatality of so many boys. Not that they expected to go to war and descend into the trenches and fire hail-storms of steel-coated death-messengers at the enemy. Oh, no. They might, but they were sensible enough not to let their imagination carry them so far. But preparedness was in the air, and the girls voted to a—a—girl (I almost said man, for they were as brave as men in many respects) to take up military drill and tactics two hours a week as a part of their curriculum.

Madame Cleaver, head of the Institute, did not start the military movement rashly. She was carefully diplomatic in the conduct of her school, for she must satisfy the critical tastes and ideas of a high-class parentage clientele. But she also kept her fingers on the pulse of affairs and knew pretty well how to strike a popular vein. Hence the membership of her classes was always on the increase. Indeed, at the beginning of this school year, she had to turn away something like forty applicants, for want of room and accommodations.

Hiawatha Institute was founded as a Camp Fire Girls' school, and when Uncle Sam became involved in the European war, the national need for nurses appealed strongly to Camp Fire Girls everywhere. What could they do? The very nature of the training of the girls from Wood Gatherer to Torch Bearer made the question, so far as they were concerned, a self-answering one. They had all the broad commonsense rudiments of nursing. With some advanced science on top of this, they would be experts.

But military authorities said that the nurses ought to have some military drill. War nurses must be organized, and there was no better method of effecting this orderly requisite than by military training.

One well-known captain of infantry informed Madame Cleaver that war nurses could not reach the highest grade of efficiency unless they were able to march in columns from one camp to another and be distributed in squads at the points needed.

With all this information at her tongue's end, the madame put the matter to her uniformed girls in the assembly hall. Rumor of what was coming had reached them in advance, so that it did not fall as a surprise. The vote was unanimous in favor of the plan. The needed nursing expert was already a member of the faculty. The classes were formed a few days later.

These were the girls that gathered around a big out-door campfire—it was really a bonfire—in the snow of mid-winter on the evening of the opening of this story. Most of them were rich men's daughters, but there were no snobs among them. They were girls of vigor and vim, intelligence and imagination, practical and industrious. They were lively and fond of a good time, but—most of them, at least,—would not slight a duty for pleasure. Behind every enjoyment was a pathway of tasks well done.

Madame Cleaver was Chief Guardian of the fifteen Camp Fires of the Institute. The faculty was not large enough to supply all the adult guardians required, but that fact did not prove by any means an insurmountable difficulty. More than enough young women in Westmoreland, well qualified to fill positions of this kind, volunteered to donate their services in order to make the Camp Fire organization of the school complete. Indeed, these volunteer Guardians added materially to their influence and rank in the community by becoming connected with the Institute. There was, in fact, a waiting list of volunteers constantly among the social leaders of the place.

The Chief Guardian was mistress of ceremonies at the Grand Council Fire. Two hundred and thirty-nine girls in uniform, brown coats, campfire hats, and brown duck hiking boots, stood around the fire answering "Kolah" in unison by groups as the roll of the Fires was called. As each Fire was called and the answer returned, the Guardian stepped forward and gave a little recitation of current achievements. This program was varied here and there with music by a girls' chorus and a girls' orchestra. Everything went along with the smoothness, although with some of the deep dips and lofty lifts, of Grand Opera, until the name of the last Camp Fire, Flamingo, was called. Miss Harriet Ladd, the Guardian, stepped forward and said:

"Madame Chief Guardian, associate guardians, and Camp Fire Girls of Hiawatha Institute, I bring to you a message of things planned by Flamingo Camp Fire Girls, thirteen in number. As you know, there is in an adjoining state a strike of coal miners that has caused much suffering among the poor families of the strikers. High Peak lives in a mountain mining district. Her father is a mine owner and has given his consent to the extending of an invitation to Flamingo Camp Fire to work among these poor families and give them relief during the Christmas holidays. The arrangements have been completed, and the girls will start for Hollyhill tomorrow."

"Hooray, hooray, hooray! Hooray for High Peak! Hooray for Marion Stanlock! Hooray for Flamingo Camp Fire."

The cheers, shrill on the sharp winter air, now in unison, now in confusion, came not from the assembled Camp Fire Girls, although from nearly as many voices. Out from the timber thicket to the west of the campus rushed a small army of khaki-clad figures. There were a few screams among the girls, but not many. To be sure, everybody was thrilled, but nobody fainted. There were a few moments of suspense, followed by bursts of laughter and applause from the girls.

"It's the Spring Lake Boy Scouts," cried Marion Stanlock, who was first to announce an explanation of the surprise. "Clifford, Clifford Long, are you responsible for this?"

The Boy Scout patrol leader thus addressed did not reply, though he recognized the challenge with a wave of his hand.

He was busy bringing his patrol in matching line with the other patrols. As if realizing their purpose, the circle around the camp fire was broken at a point nearest the newly arrived invaders, and an avenue of approach was formed by the lining up of some of the girls in two rows extended out towards the Boy Scouts. In double file a hundred and fifty boys marched in and around the campfire; then faced toward the outer ring of Camp Fire Girls and bowed acknowledgment of the courteous reception.

CHAPTER II

THE BOY SCOUTS' INVASION

That was a grand surprise that the Boy Scouts of Spring Lake academy "put over" on the Camp Fire Girls of Hiawatha Institute. They had been planning it for several weeks, or since they first received information of the Grand Council Fire as a closing event of the first semester of the girls' school. The two institutions were located in municipalities only fifteen miles apart, connected by both steam railroad and electric interurban lines.

Spring Lake academy, located on a lake of the same name at the southern outskirt of Kingston, was originally a boys' military school, and it still retained that primal distinction. But the success of Hiawatha Institute as a Camp Fire Girls' school set the imaginative minds of some of the leaders of the boys at Spring Lake to work along similar lines, with the result that the faculty's cooperation was petitioned for the organization of the student body into a troop of Boy Scout patrols. The scheme was successful, and as it served to inject new life into the academy, the business end of the institution had no ground for complaint.

This innovation at Spring Lake was due largely to the activities of Clifford Long, one of the students. He was a cousin of Marion Stanlock, and naturally this relationship served to direct his personal interest toward Hiawatha Institute. Not a few other students in these two schools were similarly related, some of them being brothers and sisters.

And so it is not to be wondered at if these two places of learning became, as it were, twin schools, with much of interest in common and many of their activities interassociated. They had rival debating teams between which were held more or less periodic contests, and in the numerous social events there were frequently exchanges of invitational courtesies.

The boys plotted their big surprise on the girls in true scout fashion. There was no real secret in the fact that the Camp Fire Girls of Hiawatha Institute were planning a big event, but girl-like they affected secrecy to stimulate interest. The result was more than could have been expected, although the girls did not realize this until after it was all over. The curiosity of the Spring Lake boys was thoroughly alive as soon as they learned of a mysterious "something big" going on at the institute. True to the character of real scouts they delegated emissaries, commonly denominated spies, to visit the stronghold of the Camp Fire Girls, get all the details of their plans discoverable and report back to headquarters. Greater success than that which rewarded their efforts could hardly have been wished for. Half a dozen boys went and returned and then put their heads and their reports together with the result that the Scouts of the school had all the information they needed.

They mapped out their plans and scheduled their prospective movements by the calendar and the clock. They chartered an interurban train for the run to and from the Institute. The arrival on the scene of the Grand Council Fire was, as we have seen, a complete surprise to the girls. The Scouts well knew that their presence would not be regarded as an intrusion, for a Grand Council Fire, according to the handbook, "is for friends and the public."

The interruption of the program by the marching of the Boy Scouts within the circle of the Camp Fire Girls was permitted to continue for ten or fifteen minutes, while a number of short speeches were made by some of the boy leaders, in which they gloried over the way they had "put one over on the girls."

"And we're not through yet," announced Harry Gilbert prophetically. "Some of us are going to put over another surprise just about as thrilling as this, and we want to challenge you to find out what it is."

Of course this statement produced the very result the boys desired. Naturally they wished the girls to think they were pretty bright fellows. They got just what they were looking for as a result of their "surprise," namely, volumes of praise. To be sure, this did not come in the form of undisguised admiration. That isn't the way a clever girl signifies her approval of this sort of thing. It just burst into evidence through such mock jeers as, "You boys think you are so smart," or "It's a wonder you wouldn't have gone to enough pains to build a railroad or sink a submarine."

To which, on one occasion in the course of the evening, Earl Hamilton replied:

"Thank you, ladies; we always do things thorough."

"-ly!" screamed Katherine Crane. Yes, it was really a scream, an explosion, too, if the indelicacy may be excused. But the opportunity for a come-back struck her so keenly, so swiftly, that she just could not contain her eagerness to beat somebody else to it.

Well, the laugh that followed also was of the nature of an explosion. And it was on poor Katherine quite as much as on Earl, who had tripped up on an adjective in place of an adverb. The girl's eagerness was so evident that it struck everybody as funnier than the boy's mistake in grammar. Anyway, she recovered quite smartly and followed up her attack with this pert addendum as the laughter subsided:

"You evidently don't do your lessons thorough-ly." The emphasis on the "-ly" was so pronounced, almost spasmodic, as to bring forth another laughing applause.

This exchange of repartee took place in the large school auditorium, to which all repaired as soon as the outdoor exercises had been finished.

The program of the evening was punctuated by interruptions of this kind every now and then. Of course, the fun-makers waited for suitable opportunities to spring their "quips and cranks," so that no merited interest in the doing could be lost. And none of it was lost. The presence of the bold invaders seemed to add zest to the most routine of the Camp Fire performances, and when all was over everybody was agreed that there had not been a dull minute during the whole evening.

At the close of the Camp Fire Girls' program the 150 Boy Scouts arose and, with heroic unison of voices peculiar to much practice in the delivery of school yells, they chanted a clever parody of Wo-he-lo Cheer, a Boy Scout's compliment to the Camp Fire Girls, and then marched out of the auditorium and away toward the interurban line, where their chartered train was waiting for them, and all the while they continued the chant with variations of the words, the rhythmic drive of their voices pulsing back to the Institute, but becoming fainter and more faint until at last the sound was lost with the speeding away of the trolley train in the distance.

CHAPTER III

THE SKULL AND CROSS-BONES

If Marion Stanlock, "High Peak" in the trait and a torch bearer, had read one of two letters, signed with a "skull and cross-bones," which she found lying on the desk in her room after the adjournment of the Grand Council Fire, doubtless there would have been an interruption, and probably a change, in the holiday program of the Flamingo Camp Fire. She saw the letters lying there and under ordinary circumstances would have torn them open and read them, however hastily, before retiring. But on this occasion she was rather tired, owing to the activities and the excitement of the day and evening. Moreover, she realized that she could not hope for anything but a wearisome journey to Hollyhill on the following day unless she refreshed herself with as many hours sleep as possible before train time.

So she merely glanced at the superscriptions on the envelopes to see if the letters were from any of her relatives or friends, and, failing to recognize either of them, she put them into her handbag, intending to read them at the first opportunity next morning. Then she went to bed and fell asleep almost instantly.

Marion was awakened in the morning by her roommate, Helen Nash, who had quietly arisen half an hour earlier. The latter was almost ready for breakfast when she woke her friend from a sleep that promised to continue several hours longer unless interrupted. She had turned on the electric light and was standing before the glass combing her hair. Marion glanced at the clock to see what time it was, but the face was turned away from her and the light in the room made it impossible for her to observe through the window shades that day was just breaking.

"What time is it, Helen?" she asked. "Did the alarm go off? I didn't hear it. What waked you up?"

Helen did not answer at once. For a moment or two her manner seemed to indicate that she did not hear the questions of the girl in bed. Then, as if suddenly rescuing her mind from thoughts that appealed to have carried her away into some far distant abstraction, she replied thus, in a series of disconnected utterances:

"No, the alarm didn't go off—a—Marion. I got up at 6 o'clock. I turned the alarm off. It is 6:30 now. I don't know what woke me. I just woke up."

Marion arose, wondering at the peculiar manner of her roommate and the strained, almost convulsive, tone of her voice. She asked no further questions, but proceeded with her dressing and preparation for breakfast. For the time being, she forgot all about the two letters in her handbag that lay on her dresser.

In some respects Helen was a peculiar girl. If her speech and action had been characterized with more vim, vigor and imagination, doubtlessly she would generally have been known as a pretty girl. As it was, her features were regular, her complexion fair, her eyes blue, and her hair a light brown. Marion thought her pretty, but Marion had associated with her intimately for two or three years, and had discovered qualities in her that mere acquaintances could never have discovered. She had found Helen apparently to be possessed of a strong, direct conception of integrity, never vacillating in manner or sympathies. Moreover, she exhibited a quiet, unwavering capability in her work that always commanded the respect, and occasionally the admiration, of both classmates and teachers.

Not only was Helen quiet of disposition, but strangely secretive on certain subjects. For instance, she seldom said anything about her home or relatives. She lived in Villa Park, a small town midway between Westmoreland and Hollyhill. Her father was dead, and, when not at school, she had lived with her mother; these two, so far as Marion knew, constituting the entire family.

Marion had visited her home, and there found the mother and daughter apparently in moderate circumstances. Naturally, she had wondered a little that Mrs. Nash should be able to support her daughter at a private school, even though that institution made a specialty of teaching rich men's daughters how to be useful and economical, but the reason why had never been explained to her. Helen got her remittances from home regularly, and seemed to have no particular cause to worry about finances. She had spent parts of two vacations at the Stanlock home and there conducted herself as if quite naturally able to fit in with luxurious surroundings and large accommodations.

Only a few days before the Christmas holidays, something had occurred that emphasized Helen's secretive peculiarity to such an extent that Marion was considerably provoked and just a little mystified. A young man, somewhere about 25 or 27 years old, fairly well but not expensively dressed, and bearing the appearance of one who had seen a good deal of the rough side of life, called at the Institute and asked for Miss Nash. He was ushered into the reception room and Helen was summoned. One of the girls who witnessed the meeting told some of her friends that Miss Nash was evidently much surprised, if not unpleasantly disturbed, when she recognized her caller. Immediately she put on a coat and hat and she and the young man went out. An hour later she returned alone, and to no one did she utter a word relative to the stranger's visit, not even to her roommate, who had passed them in the hall as they were going out.

Helen Nash was a member of the Flamingo Camp Fire and accompanied the other members on their vacation trip to the mountain mining district. The other eleven who boarded the train with Marion, the holiday hostess, were Ruth Hazelton, Ethel Zimmerman, Ernestine Johanson, Hazel Edwards, Azalia Atwood, Harriet Newcomb, Estelle Adler, Julietta Hyde, Marie Crismore, Katherine Crane, and Violet Munday.

Miss Ladd, the Guardian, also was one of Marion's invited guests. The party took possession of one end of the parlor car, which, fortunately, was almost empty before they boarded it. Then began a chatter of girl voices—happy, spirited, witty, and promising to continue thus to the end of the journey, or until their kaleidoscopic subjects of conversation were exhausted.

Every thrilling detail of the evening before was gone over, examined, given its proper degree of credit, and filed away in their memories for future reference. There was more catching of breath, more cheering, more clapping of hands; but no mock jeers, now that the boys were absent, as the events of the Boy Scouts' invasion and the many incidental and brilliant results were recalled and repictured.

"I wonder what Harry Gilbert meant when he said some of them were planning another surprise nearly as thrilling as the one they sprung last night," said Azalia Atwood, with characteristic excitable expectation. "He addressed himself to you, Marion, when he said it; and he's a close friend of your cousin, Clifford Long. Whatever it is, I bet anything it will fall heaviest on this Camp Fire when it comes."

"Maybe it was just talk, to get us worked up and looking for something never to come," suggested Ethel Zimmerman. "It would be a pretty good one for the boys to get us excited and looking for something clear up to April 1, and then spring an April fool joke, something like a big dry goods box packed with excelsior."

"Oh, but that wouldn't measure up to expectations," Ruth Hazelton declared. "It wouldn't be one-two-three with what they did last night, and they promised something just about as interesting."

"You don't get me," returned Ethel. "The dry goods box filled with excelsior would be the anti-climax of wondering expectations."

"You're too deep for a twentieth century bunch of girls, Ethel," Hazel Edwards objected. "That might easily be mistaken for the promised big stunt. They might compose a lot of ditties and mix them up with the packing, something like this:

"'Believe not all big things that boys may tell thee, for

Great expectations may produce excelsior'."

"Very clever, indeed, only it sounds like an impossible combination of Alice in Wonderland and an old maid," said Harriet Newcomb, with a toss of her head. "I'm surprised at you, Hazel, for suggesting such a thing. If the boys should put over anything like that, we'd break off diplomatic relations right away. If they wanted to call us a lot of rummies, they couldn't do it as effectively by the use of direct language. Cleverness usually makes a hit with its victims, unless it contains an element of contempt."

"That is really a brilliant observation," announced the Guardian who had been listening with quiet interest to the spirited conversation. "Continued thought along such lines ought to result in a Keda National Honor for you, Harriet."

"I'll agree to all that if Harriet will take back what she said about my being an old maid," said Hazel with mock dignity.

"I didn't call you an old maid, my dear," denied the impromptu poet pertly. "I merely said, or meant to say, that the idea you expressed might better be expected from an old maid, although I doubt if many old maids could have expressed it as well as you did."

"Girls, Girls, are you going to turn our vacation into a two-weeks repartee bee?" Marion broke in with affected desperation. "If you do, you will force your hostess to go way back and sit down, and that wouldn't be polite, you know. By the way, if you'll excuse me I'll do that very thing now for another reason. I've got two letters in my hand bag that I forgot all about. I'm going to read them right now. You girls are making too much chatter. I can't read in your midst."

So saying, Marion retired to a chair just far enough away to lend semblance of reality to her "go way back and sit down" suggestion, and settled back comfortably to read the two missives that arrived with the last evening's mail at the Institute.

"Settled back comfortably"—yes, but only for a short time. Marion never before in her life received two such letters. Both were anonymous. The first one that she opened aroused enough curiosity to "unsettle" her. She thought she knew whom it was from—those ingenious Boy Scouts of Spring Lake— perhaps it was written by cousin Clifford himself. It was just like him. He was a natural leader among boys, and often up to mischief of some sort. Marion was sure he was one of the prime movers of the Scout invasion of Hiawatha Institute.

But the next letter was the real thriller, or rather cold chiller. She knew very well what it meant. From the point of view of the writer it meant "business," a threat well calculated to work terror in her own heart and the heart of every other member of Flamingo Fire. It was a threat couched in direful words, warning her and her friends not to go to Hollyhill on their charity mission, as announced, and predicting serious injury if not death to some of them. It was signed with a skull and cross-bones.

CHAPTER IV

STUDYING THE MYSTERY

Is there any wonder that Marion Stanlock, after reading letter No. 2 was seriously in doubt as to whether No. 1 was from the Scouts who had promised another surprise for the Camp Fire Girls in the near future? Judge for yourself—here is No. 1:

Something Doing Soon

Look Out

SOMETHING DOING SOON

LOOK OUT

SOMETHING DOING SOON

LOOK OUT!

That was all. The second letter read thus:

"Miss Stanlock: This is to serve you with warning not to take your friends with you to Hollyhill this vacation to work among the poor families of the striking miners. We know that move of yours is inspired by the rankest hypocrisy, that you have no genuine desire to do anything for our starving families. This move of yours, we know, was planned by that villainous father of yours to cloud the big issue of our fight. If you do carry out your plans, some of you are liable to get hurt, and it need not surprise anybody if some of you never get back to Westmoreland alive.

Go Slow! Be Careful! Look Out!"

Marion was not easily panic-stricken, but it is of the nature of a truism to say that this letter applied the severest test to her nerves. That the writer was in deep earnest she had no reason to doubt. She had read of so many crimes preceded by threatening letters of this sort that the suggestion did not come to her to regard this one lightly. Although there was no common basis for comparing the handwriting of the two missives, one being lettered in Roman capitals and the other in ordinary script, nevertheless she quickly dismissed the first suspicion that letter No. 1 was written by Clifford Long or some other Scout of Spring Lake academy. Both ended with the words "Look Out." Plainly this was a result of carelessness on the part of the writer.

Evidently he had planned to cause her to believe that the two letters were written by different persons, for he had taken the pains of differentiating the superscriptions on the envelopes as well as the contents within.

But now the question was, What should she do? It was no more than fair and just for her to inform the girls what they might expect if they attempted to carry out their original plan, but what method should she pursue to convey to them this information? She might go at the matter bluntly and create something of a panic; then again she might so handle it that the best possible result could be obtained in a quiet and orderly manner.

Marion felt in this crisis that a great responsibility rested on her to handle the problem with all the skill and intelligence at her command. She longed for the counsel of an older and more experienced head, but there was none present, except Miss Ladd, the Guardian of the Fire, to whom she might go with her story. The latter, though she came well within the requirements of the national board to fill the position which she held, was nevertheless a young woman in the sensitive sense of the phrase and could hardly be expected to give the best of executive advice under the circumstances. Marion realized that it was her duty to exhibit to Miss Ladd the letters she had received, but if she did this at once, the act would amount to turning the whole matter over to her and relinquishing the initiative herself, she reasoned.

Marion was naturally aggressive, and she was not favorably impressed with the idea of leaving the affair in the hands of another unless that person were peculiarly fitted to handle it. As she sat studying over the problem she suddenly became conscious of the presence of another person close beside her, and looking up she saw Helen Nash, with an expression of startled intelligence in her eyes. Apparently her attention had been attracted by the crude drawing of a skull and cross-bones at the close of the letter lying open in her lap.

"I beg your pardon, Marion," said Helen with an evident effort at self-control. "I didn't mean to intrude. I hope you'll forgive me for something quite unintentional."

"Certainly, Helen," Marion replied generously, "and since a chance look has informed you of the nature of these letters and I want to talk this affair over with somebody, I think I may as well talk it over with you. Let's go down to the other end of the car where we aren't likely to be disturbed."

Accordingly they moved up to the front of the car where they took possession of two chairs and soon were so deeply absorbed in the problem at hand as to excite the wonder and curiosity of the other Camp Fire Girls.

Marion handed the two anonymous letters to her friend without introductory remark, and the latter read them. As Marion watched the expression on the reader's face, she was forced to admit to herself that right then, under those seemingly impersonal circumstances, Helen's habitual strangeness of manner was more pronounced than she had ever before known it to be. This girl of impenetrable secrecy read the letters, seemingly with an abstraction amounting almost to inattention, while physically she appeared to shrink from something that to her alone was visible and real.

As she finished reading, Helen looked up at her friend and the gaze of penetrating curiosity that she saw in Marion's eyes caused her to blush with confusion. Unable to meet her friend's gaze steadily, she shifted her eyes toward the most uninteresting part of the car, the floor, and said:

"That looks like a dangerous letter. It ought to be turned over to the police as soon as possible."

"Both of them, don't you think?" Marion inquired.

"Why? I don't see anything in this shorter one. My guess would be that it was written by your cousin or one of his friends."

"But do you notice the way they both end?—the same words," Marion insisted.

"Yes, I noticed that," Helen replied slowly. But that is such a common, ordinary expression, almost like 'a,' 'an,' or 'the,' that it doesn't mean much to me here. Where are the letters postmarked?"

"Both in Westmoreland."

"That's something in favor of your suspicion that both letters were written by the same person," Helen admitted. "Still it doesn't convince me. You wouldn't expect the Spring Lake boys to mail a letter like the shorter one at Spring Lake, would you? That would stamp its identity right away."

"You are sure those letters were written by different persons?" Marion inquired curiously.

"I don't think it makes any difference whether they were or not," Helen answered more decisively than she had spoken before. "It is in that skull-and-cross-bones letter that you are most interested. I think you can disregard the other entirely. I would say this, however, that if both were written by one person, you have less to fear than if the shorter one was written by your cousin or one of his friends."

"Why?"

"Because if one person wrote both of them, he is probably suffering from softening of the brain. But if the person who wrote the longer one did not write the shorter one, there is more likelihood that he means business and will attempt to carry out his threat."

"I never realized that you were such a Sherlock Holmes," Marion exclaimed enthusiastically, while the suggestion came to her that perhaps a genius for this sort of thing accounted for her friend's peculiarities. "You ought to be a detective for a department store to catch shoplifters."

"Thanks, Marion, for the compliment, but I am not inclined that way. I'd rather do something in this case to keep our vacation plans from ending in trouble."

"I was looking for someone who could advise me," Marion said; "and I am now convinced that you are just the person I was looking for. What do you think I ought to do, Helen?"

"All the girls ought to know about this letter," Helen replied. "But you can't go to them and blurt out anything so sensational. We must break the news gently, as they say in melodrama. I wish we hadn't come."

"So do I," Marion replied, but with just a suggestion of disappointment in her voice.

"Not that I am afraid of getting hurt," Helen added hastily, realizing the suspicion of cowardice that might rest against her. "Still, if my advice had been asked, I would have argued against this very dangerous vacation scheme of yours."

"Why?" inquired Marion in a tone of disappointment.

"Because of the very situation complained of in that skull-and-cross-bones letter. I hope I don't hurt your feelings, Marion, but it is very natural for some of these rough miners to suspect that your plan was cooked up by your father to pull the wool over their eyes, and to regard you as a tool employed by him to put the scheme into operation."

"Some of the girls' parents raised the objection that there might be danger in a mining district during a strike, but none of them suggested anything of this sort," Marion remarked with humble anxiety. "I explained to them that there could hardly be any danger even if the strikers should get ugly, as the mines are some distance from where we live and any violence on the part of the miners would surely be committed at the scene of their labors. This seemed to satisfy them. Most of the miners live at the south end of the town or along the electric line running from Hollyhill to the mines."

"That doesn't make much difference if the miners once get it into their heads that the girls are being used to put over a confidence game on them," Helen argued authoritatively. "Miners are peculiar people, especially if they are lead by radical leaders of aggressive purpose. They believe that they are a badly misused set, turning out the wealth of the wealthy, who repay them by holding them in contempt, keeping their wages down to a minimum and pressing them into social and political subjection."

"Where did you learn all that, Helen?" Marion asked wonderingly. "You are not even studying sociology at school. You talk like a person of experience."

"My father was a miner," Helen began. Then she stopped, and Marion saw from the expression in her eyes and the twitch of her mouth that a big lump in her throat had interrupted her explanation. She seemed to be making an effort to continue, but was unable to do so.

"Never mind, Helen," said Marion, taking her hand tenderly in her own. "I am more convinced than ever that I found just the right person to advise me when I laid this matter before you. We will try to work this problem out together. Meanwhile we must take Miss Ladd into our confidence. Why, here she is now."

CHAPTER V

GIRLS COURAGEOUS

"What's the matter, girls? You look as if you had the weight of the world on your shoulders."

Miss Ladd spoke these words lightly as if to pass judgment on the conference as entirely too serious for a Christmas holiday occasion. Marion and Helen did not respond in tones of joviality, as might have been expected. They met her jocular reproach with expressions of such serious portent that the Guardian of the Fire could no longer look upon it as calling for words of levity.

"What's the matter, girls?" she repeated more seriously. "You look worried."

"Sit down, Miss Ladd, and read these letters I received last night," said Marion without any change of tone or manner. "They will explain the whole thing. We were just about to call you aside and lay our trouble before you."

"Trouble," Miss Ladd repeated deprecatingly, "I hope it isn't as bad as that."

She drew an upholstered armchair close to the girls and began at once to examine the letters that Marion handed to her. Marion and Helen watched her closely as she read, but the Guardian of Flamingo Fire indicated her strength of character by a stern immobility of countenance until she had finished both letters. Then she looked at Marion steadily and said inquiringly:

"I suppose you have no idea who wrote these letters?"

"Not the slightest," replied the girl addressed, "unless the shorter one was written and mailed by some of the Boy Scouts at Spring Lake. Helen thinks it was, and I am inclined to believe with her that it doesn't make much difference to us who wrote it. The other letter is the one we are most interested in."

"I agree with you thoroughly," said Miss Ladd energetically. "And we have got to do something to prevent him from carrying out his threat."

"Ought we to inform the other girls now?" asked Marion with a sense of growing courage, for she felt that in the Camp Fire's Guardian she had found elements of wise counsel extending even beyond that young woman's experience.

20

"Why, yes," Miss Ladd replied. "I see no reason for delay. I'd rather tell them now than just before or after we get to Hollyhill. If we tell them now they'll have a couple of hours in which to stiffen their courage. There are eleven girls besides you two. Suppose you call them here in three lots in succession, four, four, and three, and we'll tell them quietly what has occurred and give them a little lecture as to how they should meet this crisis."

"All right," said Marion, rising. "I'll bring the first four and you get your lecture ready."

"It's ready already," said the guardian reassuringly. "It is so simple that I have no need of preparation."

"I'm afraid I need some drill in the best means and methods of reading character," Marion told herself as she walked back to the rear of the car. "I was really afraid to take the matter up with Helen or Miss Ladd for fear lest they recommend something foolish. Now it appears that each of them has a very clever head on her shoulders. Maybe I'll find the other girls possessed of just as good qualities. If I do, this day will have brought forth an important revelation to me, that the average girl, after all, is a pretty level-headed sort of person. Well, here's hoping for the best."

Marion selected the four girls farthest in front and asked them to approach the forward end of the car. They did so with some appearance of apprehension, for by this time all the girls had begun to suspect that something unusual was doing. This appeared to be evident also to the half-dozen other passengers in the car, whose curious attention naturally was directed toward the forward group of girls.

All of the girls received the information relative to the anonymous letters so calmly that Marion felt just a little bit foolish because of her groundless misjudgment of them. After the last group had read the letters and discussed the situation with the trio of informants, she spoke thus to them:

"Girls, you are real heroines, or have in you the stuff that makes heroines, and that is about the same thing. You take this as calmly as if it were an ordinary every-day affair in the movies. I'm proud of you."

"We ought to be wearing Carnegie medals, oughtn't we, girls?" said Julietta Hyde, blinking comically. "We can throttle anything from a black-hand agent to a ghost."

"No, you ought to be wearing honor pins, for things well done," Miss Ladd corrected. "We'll leave the Carnegie medals for those who haven't any Camp Fire scheme of honors. But really, girls, you have all conducted yourselves admirably in this affair. We will hope it won't result in anything very serious, but meanwhile we must take proper precautions."

"Shall we have to give up our vacation at Hollyhill on account of this?" asked Katherine Crane almost as dejectedly as if she were being sentenced to prison for violating a Connecticut blue law.

"That is up to you girls and the conditions that develop," answered Miss Ladd. "As soon as we get to Hollyhill we will take the matter up with the proper authorities and try to determine what the outlook is."

"My father will get busy as soon as he hears about this," said Marion. "I think we can leave everything to his management. He will probably advise us to give up the idea of doing anything for the strikers' families and have as good a time as we can entertaining ourselves at home."

"Oh, I hope not!" Katherine exclaimed, and the manner in which she spoke indicated how much she had set her heart on the work they had planned to do.

"It would be too bad to give it up," Marion said earnestly, "for I understand some of those people are greatly in need of assistance. There is not only much hunger and privation among them, but considerable sickness among the children. We can't do a whole lot in two weeks, but we can do something, and our training as Camp Fire Girls and in our nursing classes fits us to be of much assistance to them. It is a shame that they should take an attitude so hostile to their own interests."

"They probably don't understand your father or they wouldn't be striking now," said Miss Ladd.

"I'm sure they wouldn't," Marion testified vigorously. "I've often heard father say he'd like to do more for the men and their families but conditions tied his hands. Many of the miners are good fellows, but they get mistaken ideas in their heads and it's impossible for anybody whom they once put under suspicion to convince them that they are in the wrong."

"Do you know, girls," interposed Violet Munday enthusiastically; "I believe we are going to get a lot out of this vacation experience, whatever happens. I'm interested in what Marion tells us about the miners. Let's make a study of coal mining, hold up everybody we can for information and watch our chance to help the poor families and their sick children whenever we can without doing anything foolhardy."

"That's a good idea," said Miss Ladd. "We'll keep that in mind and if Marion's father's advice is favorable, we'll take it up."

The train arrived at Hollyhill shortly after 2 p.m. Mr.Stanlock's touring car and two taxicabs were waiting at the station to convey the girls to Marion's home. The run to the spacious, half-rustic Stanlock residence at the northeast edge of the city occupied about fifteen minutes, and was without notable incident.

The cars passed through a massive iron gateway, up a winding gravel-bedded drive, and stopped near a white pillared pergola connected with the large colonial house by a vine-covered walk running up to a porticoed side entrance.

Mrs.Stanlock met them at the door and the travelers were speedily accommodated with the usual journey-end attentions. Marion then inquired

for her father, but Mr.Stanlock had gone to his office early in the day and would not return until dinnertime. So the girl hostess decided that she must let the problem uppermost in her mind rest unsettled a few hours longer.
Evening came, but still Mr.Stanlock did not appear. Wondering at his delay, Mrs.Stanlock called up his office, but learned that he had left an hour and a half before, supposedly for home.
"How did he leave?" Mrs.Stanlock inquired nervously.

"In his automobile," was the answer.

That being the case, he ought to have been home more than an hour ago. His office was in the city and he could easily make the run in fifteen minutes.

Thoroughly alarmed, Mrs.Stanlock called up the police, stated the circumstances and asked that a search be made for her husband.

Two hours more elapsed and the whole neighborhood was alarmed. The news spread rapidly and was communicated by phone to most of Mr.Stanlock's friends and acquaintances throughout the city. The search was growing in scope and sensation. Treachery was suspected, a tragedy was feared.

Then suddenly and calmly, Mr.Stanlock reappeared at home, driving the machine himself. He had a thrilling story to tell of his experiences.

CHAPTER VI

THE PUNSTER MAKES A FIND

When Marion Stanlock selected the term High Peak as her Camp Fire name, her deliberations carried her back from Hiawatha Institute to the scene of most of the years of her child life in Hollyhill. Confronted with the task of choosing a name, she first consulted her ideals to determine what associations she wished to have in mind when in after years she recalled the motive and circumstances of her selection.

Home surroundings had always had much of beauty for Marion. From the beginning of his business career, Mr.Stanlock had had a large income and was able to supply his family with many of the expensive luxuries, as well as all the so-called necessities of life. But for Marion the artificial luxuries had little special attraction. She accepted them as a matter of course, but that is about all the claim they had upon her. She enjoyed the use of her father's automobiles, but she wondered sometimes at the scheme of things which entitled her to an electric runabout or a limousine and a chauffeur, while thousands of other quite as deserving girls were not nearly as well favored.

The ability and the disposition to look at things occasionally from this point of view contributed much to the generosity of Marion's nature. She was a favorite among rich and poor alike, except among those rich who could "understand" why the wealthy ought to be specially favored, and those poor too narrow and circumscribed to credit any wealthy person with genuine generosity.

Being of this artless and unartificial trend of mind, Marion must naturally turn to either nature or human merit for the selection of her Camp Fire name. She was not sufficiently mature to pick a poetic idea from the achievements of men, and so it fell to nature to supply a quaint notion as a foundation for her "nom-de-fire."

Seated in her room at Hiawatha Institute one evening, Marion cast about her mental horizon for some scene or association in her life that would suggest the desired name. The first that came to her was the picture of a towering mountain, conspicuous not so much for its actual loftiness as for its deceptive appearance of great height. In all her experiences at home, it had never occurred to Marion to think of this individual portion of prehistoric geologic upheaval as a mass of earth and stones. She thought of it only as the most beautiful expression of nature she had ever seen, graceful of form, rich in the seasons' decorations.

This mountain was probably about as slender as it is possible for a mountain to be. Compared, or contrasted, with a nearby and characteristic mountain of the range, it was as a lady's finger to a telescoped giant's thumb. High Peak, as the tapering sugar-loaf of earth was called, was located west of Hollyhill, close to the town. In fact the portion of the city inhabited by the main colony of miners' families was built on the sloping ground that formed a foothill of the mountain.

And so when Marion named herself as a Camp Fire Girl after this mountain she had in mind an ideal expressed in the first injunction of the Law of the Camp Fire, which is to

"Seek Beauty."

High Peak was her ideal of beauty and grandeur. It stood also, with her, for lofty aspiration. Thus she pictured the physical representation of the name she chose as a member of the great army of girls who seek romance, beauty, and adventure in every-day life.

On the day when the Flamingo Camp Fire arrived at Hollyhill, another train pulled in at the principal station several hours earlier. It came from the same direction and might, indeed, have borne the thirteen girls and their guardian if they had seen fit to get up early enough to catch a 3 o'clock train.

But the thirteen girls would have been much interested if they could have beheld the eight boy passengers as they got off in a group and looked around to see if there was anyone at the depot who knew any of them.

Relieved at the apparent absence of anybody who might recognize the one of their number whose home was in Hollyhill or another who had been a frequent visitor there, the eight boys hastened to a corner half a square away from the depot and boarded a street car that was waiting for the time to start from this terminal point. The car started almost immediately after they had seated themselves, moving in a southwesterly direction through the business section of the city and then directly west toward High Peak, passing along the northern border of the mining colony and then making a curve to the north through a more prosperous residence district.

The eight boys all wore Scout uniforms. They were the full membership of one Spring Lake patrol, the leader of which was Ernest Hunter, whose home was in Hollyhill, and who had invited all the Scouts of his patrol to be his guests during the holidays. This invitation followed the receipt of information that Marion Stanlock had invited the members of her Camp Fire to spend the Christmas holidays with her.

Ernest Hunter was well prepared to entertain his guests in real scout fashion. His parents' home was not large enough to afford sleeping quarters and other ordinary conveniences for seven visitors in addition to the regular personnel of the family, but the boy had taken care of this deficiency long before he had ever dreamed that it might occur. The Hunter home included a large tract of land running clear up to the foot of the mountain, which, at this point, was rocky and covered with a plentiful growth of white pine, hemlock and black spruce. Hidden behind an irregular heap of boulders and a small timber foreground was a cave, formed by nature and nature's anarchistic elements, that could not fail to delight the most fastidious wonder-seeker. The entrance was about the size of an ordinary doorway, flanked by twin boulders like columns for an arched shelter. Within was a large room with fairly smooth walls and ceiling of Silurian rock and sandstone.

The cave as it now appeared would hardly have been recognized by its aboriginal frequenters. It had been converted into a place of civil abode or resort, retaining only enough of its pristine wildness for romantic effect. Ernie Hunter had done his work well. He had provided for heat for the cave by running a galvanized stovepipe up through a crevice in the rocks and filling with stones and cement all the surrounding vents to guard against the draining in of water from the mountain side. He also collected and stored at home a supply of old mattresses, blankets, kitchen utensils, a laundry stove, and other domestic conveniences usable in a place of this kind. A week before vacation he wrote thus to his 12-year-old brother, Paul:

"I'm going to bring seven boys home with me. We are going to spend the vacation in the mountains, with the cave as headquarters. Will you have the stove hauled there and set up and keep a fire in it a good deal of the time to dry the place out thoroughly? We will come to Hollyhill on an early train, so as to have plenty of time to haul the mattresses and other outfittings to the cave and get it ready for habitation. We will all have guns and will have some great times shooting game. Of course, you will be in on all this."

Paul did as requested. When the patrol arrived at the Hunter home, he reported to his brother that the latter's instructions had been carried out and all was in readiness for the removal of the outing outfit from the storeroom over the garage to the cave. Everything but the mattresses were piled into Mr. Hunter's seven-passenger touring car, the eight boys piled in on top and the first run to their holiday headquarters was made.

As the machine drove up toward the mouth of the cave, the boys were startled at seeing two rough looking men emerge from the entrance and slink away to the south, half hidden by the unevenness of the ground and the thick shrubbery. Their hurried movements and evident desire to avoid meeting the boys marked them as suspicious characters. Fearing that they might have committed some malicious act to render the place uninhabitable, Ernie hastened toward the cave, followed by the other boys, to make an inspection.

Before entering, however, Ernie, who was the patrol leader, asked four of the boys to return and watch the automobile. Division of the patrol with this in view was quickly arranged, and Ernie, Clifford Long, Harry, Gilbert, and Jerry McCracken proceeded into the cave.

The entrance of the cave was protected against the cold by a heavy blanket hung over a pole anchored at either end in the rocky side at the top. Pushing aside this wilderness portiere, the four investigators stepped in, lighting their way with two or three electric flash lights.

They were relieved to discover that no damage had been done to the cave or to the stove set up within. After satisfying themselves on this score they proceeded to replenish the fire, by putting in several cuts of spruce, a good supply of which had been provided by Ernie's brother. The cave was still warm and had been well dried out by the steady fire kept up by Paul for two or three days.

The entire patrol now reassembled and mapped out a plan for completing their day's work. It was decided that Ernie should return in the automobile to his home a mile and a half away and bring the mattresses and a supply of food that was being prepared for them at the house, while the others took upon themselves the task of cutting a supply of brushwood to lay on the floor of the cave as a kind of spring support for the mattresses. Accordingly Ernie got into the machine and drove away, while the other boys got busy with the task assigned to them.

The patrol leader returned, in less than an hour, accompanied by Paul and a farm hand employed by Mr. Hunter. They brought with them not only four mattresses, but the shotguns and rifles shipped by the boys from the academy for their mid-winter hunting. Ernie announced that their trunks and valises also had arrived and that George, the farm hand, would return for them in the automobile.

The work progressed rapidly and by the time the trunks and valises arrived the mattresses were all in position, the food and cooking utensils were stored away in the narrowest compass of space that could be arranged for them and a large pile of resinous wood had been gathered.

It was now 4 o'clock and the boys felt that they were entitled to a rest. A large boulder with a flat end two and a half feet in diameter was rolled into the cave and propped into position, with slabs of stone for a table. On this was placed a large kerosene lamp, which, when burning, lighted up the cave very well. A supply of camp chairs had been brought with the first load, so that everybody had a seat.

"I call this something swell, from the point of view of a smart rustic who hasn't absorbed any city nonsense," observed Miles Berryman, seating himself comfortably in a chair and gazing about with great satisfaction. "I think, Ernie, that we must all agree that you are a very wide-awake opportunist."

"Is that the kind of musician who plays an opportune at every opportunity?" inquired John St. John in a tone of gravity as deep as the cavern in which they were housed.

"Now, see here, Johnnie Two Times," exclaimed Miles portentously: "you know what we came near doing to you six months ago for springing that kind of stuff."

"We came near ducking him in the lake," reminded Earl Hamilton.

"Yes," continued Miles in the attitude of a stage threat, "and if we can't find a lake around here we can find a deep snowdrift to throw him into."

"I wonder if he catches the drift of that argument," said Clifford Long, with a wink at Miles.

"He not only catches it, but he understands, and hence he does snow drift (does know drift) of what the menacing Miles means," declared John, who had long answered to the nickname of "Johnnie Two Times," because of the combination of baptismal and family names by which he was legally known.

A roar of pun-protesting groans filled the cavern, and as several of the boys arose in attitudes of vengeance, the punster made a dive for the exit and disappeared beyond the blanket portiere. None of the protestors followed. They did not feel like engaging in any vigorous sport following the strenuous exercises they had had.

Five minutes later "Johnnie Two Times" returned. One glance at his face was sufficient guarantee that he had lost all his punning facetiousness. He held in his hand a bit of paper which he laid on the stone table by the lamp.

"Read that, boys!" he exclaimed, excitedly. "I found it outside. Those men must have dropped it. They're after Mr.Stanlock—going to hold him up."

The ten other boys needed no second bidding. They crowded around so eagerly that nobody could read.

"Here, I'll read it aloud," said Clifford, picking up the paper and holding it close to the lamp. Here is what he read:

"I will bring Old Stanlock along the foothill pike. Will slow up in the sand stretch. Be there ready to grab him. Jake."

CHAPTER VII

TO THE RESCUE

"Boys, we've got to do something," declared Patrol Leader Ernie Hunter, breaking the gaping silence that followed the reading of the note.

"What shall we do?" asked Harry Gilbert, who was a good soldier, but no leader.

"We must go to Mr.Stanlock's rescue," Ernie replied. "There is no telling what those rascals are plotting. They may kill him if we don't get there in time to prevent it."

"It's a long hike, and we may not be able to get there in time," Paul Hunter warned.

"That means we've got to move mighty fast," Ernie said. "Boys, get your guns and a supply of shells. I hope we won't have to use them, but we'd better be well prepared. We're going to be late getting back, so you may as well grab some bread and dried beef and anything else you can find in a jiffy to eat on the way. We've got to start in three minutes. Now everybody hustle.

"Paul, you and Jerry had better run home and stay there till morning," Ernie added, turning to his brother. Jerry was scarcely any larger than Paul, although the latter was a year younger. Ernie felt a slightly nervous responsibility for the safety of the "twin babies of the bunch," as some one had already referred to them in the course of the day. Jerry, who, like Paul, was an extremely likable fellow, resented being called the baby of the patrol, a term sometimes applied to him when the Scouts were dealing in jocular personalities.

"Not much are we goin' home," declared Paul, energetically; "are we, Jerry? I'm goin' along and carry my target rifle with the rest. What do you say, Jerry?"

"I'm with you," the latter announced with spirit. "They can't leave us behind."

"But you can't make the trip fast enough," Ernie insisted.

"We'll have to run part of the way, and the ground is rough, and the snow and ice on the road make it hard traveling. We've got over two miles of that kind of hiking to do, and less than an hour to do it in."

"We can make it just as well as anybody else in this bunch," declared Paul, stoutly.

"Well, come along, then; but you will have to obey orders," said Ernie, speaking as one with military authority. "We're operating under martial law tonight, and if you insist on coming along you must expect to be treated like a soldier. Everybody bring your gun and flashlight. It's cloudy now and will be dark before long."

In scarcely more time than it takes to tell it, the boys had possessed themselves of their guns, flashlights, overcoats, hats, and "a bite to eat on the run," and were dashing out along the path leading down to the road that skirted the foothill to the southward. Presently, however, they slowed down to a "dog trot" at the suggestion of Clifford Long, who warned his fellow Scouts against "tuckering themselves out."

They continued along in this manner half a mile and then, by common consent, reduced their pace to a walking long stride. As they proceeded thus, Ernie said to Clifford Long and one or two others nearest him:

"I'm afraid we've made a mistake in not doing one thing that has just occurred to me. What I ought to have done was to hurry home, got the automobile and made a race for the police station while you boys made this trip. In that way we could 'ave had a double chance of catching those bandits. If everything had gone smoothly, I might even have beaten you boys to the scene of the hold-up with an auto load of police. I could 'ave left word, too, for someone to call up Mr.Stanlock's office and warn him, if by any cause he had been delayed."

"I don't think much of that suggestion," replied Clifford; "for, if they haven't got him started by this time, they're not likely to get him going their way tonight. But the other'd 'a' been a good one. It's too bad you didn't think of it sooner."

"Too late now," said Ernie. "We've got to make the best of it."

"Who do you suppose those two men are that we saw come out of the cave?" Miles Berryman inquired.

"The chances are ninety-nine out of a hundred that this affair is connected directly with the strike," Clifford replied, with confident assurance. "The highwaymen who plotted this scheme doubtless belong to the rougher element of the strikers. They are really dangerous men, and the community would be much safer if they were lodged in prison."

"How do you suppose they got your uncle to come away out here at the time when he usually starts home for dinner—that is, if he really came this way?" asked Hal Ettelson.

"That's the very thing that's bothering me most," Clifford replied, with puzzled air. "Uncle is usually pretty shrewd, and I am pretty certain that people who try to put anything over on him generally find that they have a hard job on their hands."

"I'd take it, from the note Jerry found, that this is a decoy game they're trying to work," Ernie remarked.

"It'd have to be a sharp one to get my uncle," declared Clifford. "He's a very clever business man."

"The smartest men get caught once in a while," was Ernie's sage remark.

"That must have been a chauffeur who wrote that note," observed Johnny St. John. "It read as if a chauffeur was the brains of this plot. If we get there on time, he won't have much to chauffeur it" (show for it).

"Oh, Johnny Twice!" groaned Earl Hamilton. "Don't spoil your good deed of finding that note by springing any more of that stuff. You're taking an unfair advantage of us, for we can't stop now to duck you in a snowdrift."

The road was not broken all the way for good walking, so that the boys were forced to put forth their best efforts in order to reach the place of the plotted ambush on time.

Their pace therefore varied from a rapid walk to a run, according as their "wind" and leg muscles supplied the needed endurance. Paul and Jerry found it pretty hard to keep up with the other boys during the last three-quarters of a mile, especially when they struck a poorly broken snowdrift or a stretch of ground covered with rocks or rough ice. They were quite elated, however, at their ability to keep their feet in these rough places, after seeing two of the larger boys slip and fall.

It was almost dark by the time they reached the vicinity of the "sand stretch" referred to in the note found by "Johnny Two-Times." This stretch was a sand bed of several acres in extent, between which and High Peak was a large stone quarry. The road ran between the "sand stretch," which, of course, was now frozen and covered with snow, and the quarry. The approach to this was sheltered, fortunately for the concealment of the boy rescuers, by a growth of timber extending down the mountain slope to the road.

Ernie called a halt about two hundred yards from the point in the road which appeared the most favorable place for an ambush.

"Let's leave the road and make our way through the trees," he suggested.

"There comes the automobile!" exclaimed Paul, excitedly, pointing down the highway to the southwest.

Yes, a machine was approaching, about two miles away. The long stream of light from the electric lamps could be seen, almost hitting the sky, as the auto began to climb a steep hill. Evidently it had just turned into this highway from another thoroughfare leading direct from the city.

"Come on! We must hurry," said Ernie, dashing into the timber. "Be careful; don't fall or run any branches in your eyes."

They made fairly good progress, considering the difficulties before them and the darkness in the woods. However, they kept close to the edge, where the tree growth was not very heavy and where the snow reflected sufficient light to guide their feet. Ernie ordered that none of the flashlights be used, and perhaps it was fortunate for the success of the expedition that this order was issued and obeyed.

The efforts of the boys were well timed. Everything went like clockwork, or so it afterward seemed. Two shadowy forms were discerned standing in the thicker darkness under the trees as the automobile arrived near the Southern edge of the quarry. The boys were within easy attacking distance from the place where the two men stood. Ernie whispered the word "Halt" loud enough for his companions to hear him. They gathered around their leader, who hurriedly spoke thus:

"Now, everybody listen to me for orders. When I give the word, 'fire,' you, Paul, John, Harry and Jerry, fire your guns into the air. Be careful, and shoot up toward the tops of the trees, so as not to hit anyone. Then I'll give the order to charge, and everybody let out an Indian war-whoop or something of the sort. We won't have to do any more shooting. Now, come on; we'll get closer. Those fellows are starting now."

Even as he spoke, the two villainous individuals, with masks on their faces, dashed out from the timber and planted themselves in front of the automobile, with pistols leveled at the driver. The latter, according to the plan outlined in his note discovered by "Johnny Two-Times," slowed down the machine before the highwaymen appeared. At the command to halt he came to a sudden stop and threw up his hands.

"Ready!—Fire!" commanded Ernie in a loud voice.

Two magazine shotguns and two target rifles exploded in quick succession. Without giving the two hold-up men time to determine whether they had been hit or not, the patrol leader issued his second order, thus:

"Now, boys, after them! Charge! No quarter for the rascals!"

Then followed a scene that, for rapidity of action, is not often surpassed by motion picture speed artists.

CHAPTER VIII

THE EAVESDROPPER

If the two masked highwaymen had been crouching in position for a footrace to be started at the shot of a pistol, they could hardly have sprung forward more suddenly or have sped down the road more rapidly. One glance over their shoulders at what doubtless appeared to them to be something like a regiment of armed men was pouring out of the timber, as one of the boys afterward put it, was enough to make them "hot-foot along hot enough to melt all the ice and snow in their path."

All of the boys now produced the flashlights which they had carried in their pockets and turned them on to their own faces, in order that Mr.Stanlock might see who they were and have no doubt that they were friends. This was according to one detail of their pre-arranged plan, and worked successfully. The owner of the automobile recognized his nephew, Clifford Long, and the Scout uniforms worn by the boys, and realized at once that he had been rescued from the hands of a pair of unscrupulous rascals by a company of real boy heroes. He threw open the door, sprang out, and began shaking the hands of his rescuers in grateful appreciation of what they had done for him.

"I don't know what all this means," he said; "but I've got wits enough to understand there's been some pretty tough rascality on foot, and you boys have done me a very great service."

"We were hiking along this way and saw those two men with guns in their hands stop your machine" exclaimed Clifford, who thought it best not to reveal the discovery of the note in the presence of the chauffeur.

"You did mighty good work" declared the wealthy mine operator, enthusiastically.

"Does your Boy Scout training teach you to use your heads so successfully? One would think that this hold-up and the rescue were both plotted and planned some time ahead, judging by the skill with which you worked."

"Don't flatter us too much, uncle, or you may tempt us to help along the deception by leading you to believe that we really are a remarkable bunch of boys," Clifford warned, slyly.

"I not only believe it, but I know it," replied Mr.Stanlock with stubborn generosity. "So, if I am deceived, the fault is all my own. But, Clifford, I

35

didn't know you were in town. When did you come? You haven't been over at the house yet, have you?"

"No, not yet, uncle," Clifford answered, slowly. "And I'm not coming over for a few days. The fact is, we are here on a hunting trip and a mystery mission, and we want you to help us keep our secret. Since we have proved ourselves to be a very unusual lot of boys, perhaps you will take special care to favor us in this respect. We are planning a surprise on the girls, and we don't want you to tell them we are in town."

"My lips are sealed until you unseal them," Mr.Stanlock assured them. "But where are you staying?"

"All of us are members of one patrol of Scouts at Spring Lake Academy, all except Paul Hunter. We came here on an invitation from Ernie Hunter, and we are living in a cave at the west end of Mr. Hunter's farm."

"In a cave!" Mr.Stanlock exclaimed with some concern. "Isn't that rather an unhealthful place for you to live? You don't sleep there, I hope?"

"We certainly do, uncle; or, rather, we are going to, for this is our first night. I wish you could come over and see it. It's as dry and warm as can be. Paul dried it out by keeping a stove burning in it for several days."

"A stove in a cave!" was Mr.Stanlock's astonished comment. "That is surely some combination of wild nature and mechanical civilization. I shall certainly inspect your domesticated wild-and-woolly retreat. When am I invited to come?"

"Any time, Mr.Stanlock," Ernie interposed, with the hospitality of host. "Name your time and we'll be there to receive you."

"You'll have quite a walk to the cave tonight, and the walking isn't very good, I venture. Pile in and I'll take you in the machine."

"I'm afraid we'll make more of a load than you can carry," said Ernie.

"This machine can carry seven, nine in a pinch, and eleven in a case of life and death," assured Mr.Stanlock. "But I've got an idea that will cut off the life and death. I am bringing home a large sled that a young manual training student made for my seven-year-old son, Harold. It has a good, strong rope attached, and we will hitch it on behind, and two of you boys can ride on that."

"Let's you and me hitch," said Paul to Jerry, eagerly. Jerry was just as eager, and the problem of carrying ten passengers and the chauffeur was settled.

"One of you boys get in front with Jake and show him the way," suggested the owner of the automobile.

"Jake!" The utterance of that name sent a thrill through every one of the boys, all of whom recognized it as the name signed to the note that "Johnny Two-Times" had found near the cave.

Ernie climbed up with the driver, the sled was taken out and hitched on behind, and six of the boys "piled in" with Mr.Stanlock. As soon as Paul and Jerry called out "Go ahead," they started.

It was not quite as jolly an adventure for the two boys on the sled as they had expected. The road was pretty rough and, although the chauffeur, obeying his employer's instruction, drove carefully, the "hitchers" were twice thrown off.

But they refused to give up, declaring it to be the most fun they had had "in a coon's age," which was really a boys' bravery fib, and finally the machine drew up within a hundred and fifty feet of the cave.

The boys and Mr.Stanlock left the automobile in charge of the driver and proceeded to the Scouts' hunting headquarters. The visitor proved that he had not lost all sympathy for his youthful days, for he declared that he would like nothing better than to return to his 'teens and spend a mid-winter vacation with the young hunters in their cave. After the inspection was completed, Clifford again broached the subject of the highwaymen's attack, saying:

"Uncle, we didn't tell you how we happened to be present when those two men stopped you tonight, because we didn't want the chauffeur to hear what we had to say. The whole story is contained in this note, which one of the boys found after we had seen those men come out of the cave and hurry away. Here it is; read it. As you are more interested in it than anybody else, you may keep it."

Clifford drew the folded paper from his vest pocket and gave it to Mr.Stanlock. The latter held it close to the lamp and read.

"That's Jake, my driver; it's his handwriting I'm certain. What did be want to do that for? He must be in league with the worst element of the strikers. Probably they paid him well for this, or promised him a tempting bribe."

Mr.Stanlock mused thus aloud as he studied over the note. The situation puzzled him. What ought he to do? Of course, he must have the driver arrested, and there must be an investigation by the police. But, would it be safe for him to trust Jake to drive him home? Probably it would be safe enough, for doubtless the driver had no desire to be openly connected with the plot.

He was about decided to return home with the driver and say nothing to him about the note, when a slight noise at the entrance attracted the attention of all. Listening carefully, they could hear the sound of retreating footsteps.

"That's Jake," Mr.Stanlock exclaimed. "He overheard us. After him, or he'll run away with the machine."

The rush for the entrance threatened to cause some confusion and delay in getting out. Fortunately, however, the delay, if any, was not serious, and the pursuit soon indicated that there were some real sprinters among the boys. As they emerged from the cave, the driver was already within fifty feet of the machine. But he looked back over his shoulder and evidently thought better of his original purpose, for he turned to the left and raced down the hill toward the road at another point, leaping and striding with such recklessness that it seemed almost miraculous that he should escape a fall and serious injury.

Mr.Stanlock had no desire to attempt a capture of the traitorous chauffeur by physical force, and when he saw that Jake had given up the idea of fleeing in the automobile, he called the pursuit off. Then he announced his intention to drive the machine home himself, taking the route that led past Mr. Hunter's home. He had no fear of further trouble with the driver or his confederates, for he was certain that Jake was a coward at heart and the two highwaymen could hardly have arrived in the vicinity of the cave on foot, since they were driven off in mad haste in the opposite direction, even if they had been disposed to make another attack.

"Well, good-night, boys," he said, taking his place in the driver's seat. "You've done me a service tonight that I won't forget very soon. Come and see me, all of you, after you have sprung your surprise on the girls. I'll remember to keep your secret all right. Good night."

He put his foot on the starter, gave the steering wheel a few turns, and the throbbing machine moved over the sloping stretch of ground between the cave and the road. The boys, several of them with guns in their hands, followed him to the road and stood there ready to run to his assistance if they should see any evidences of another attack. They continued the watch for fifteen or twenty minutes, until the lights of the automobile, which pierced the darkness far ahead, indicated that he had proceeded between one and two miles without interference.

CHAPTER IX

MR STANLOCK SURPRISED

Perhaps it were better not to attempt to describe with faithfulness of detail the reception given Mr.Stanlock by his wife and family on his return home shortly before 9 o'clock that night. The fear that something of serious nature had intervened to prevent his appearing at the usual dinner hour had taken firm hold of Mrs.Stanlock, Marion, sister Kathryn, and brother Harold. The fact that the police had been searching for him for two hours or more and had been unable to make any hopeful report, had not tended in the least to relieve the tension of suspense, which became almost unbearable.

Then came the vague announcement from Mr.Stanlock's stenographer at the latter's home that he had been called away somewhere, but left no definite information. He had been called unexpectedly and left in a hurry. That was all the stenographer could say.

This information was communicated to the police, who increased the family's alarm by asking a string of questions over the telephone indicating the most direful suspicions. Had Mr.Stanlock seen or heard anything which caused him to believe that the strikers might do him bodily harm if they had an opportunity? Had he received any threatening letters? Had he appeared nervous or was there anything in his manner which indicated that he was apprehensive of trouble not already well known to the public?

Marion and her mother answered some of these questions over the telephone and half an hour later a police lieutenant called at the house and made further inquiry. There was no longer any possibility of dodging the most logical suspicions, namely, that Mr.Stanlock was the victim of a decoy plotted by some criminal element working with or under the shadow of the coal miners' strike.

And so the relief from this dread suspense was very great when he drove up to the house and walked in, smiling as if nothing unusual had happened. Marion fairly flew into her father's arms as if she had not seen him for sixteen months.

"Papa!" she cried almost hysterically; "where have you been? We've been telephoning all over the city, and the police have been searching for you for nearly two hours. Why didn't you call us up and let us know you were going to be late?"

"I was intending to call you, my dear," replied Mr.Stanlock, as he greeted her and the other members of the family with a rapid succession of hugs and kisses, indicating, in spite of his attempts to appear composed, that he had returned home not under the most ordinary circumstances.

"Why didn't you?" Marion insisted. "Do you know what a state of mind you had us in during the last two or three hours?"

"I delayed calling you because I wanted to find out how late I was going to be," Mr.Stanlock explained. "Then something happened, and I wasn't near a telephone, and something more delayed me, and I decided to come directly home without stopping on the way to telephone."

"What was it that happened, papa?" Marion demanded. "Was it anything serious?"

"Pretty serious, girlie," answered her father, pinching her cheek; "but your daddy is an awfully brave man, you know, and he can't tell his daughter any of his blood-curdling experiences unless she can listen to the roaring of cannons and the yelling of Indians without flinching."

"Now, papa, you're making fun of me," Marion protested. "Didn't anything really serious happen? The police thought you must have been waylaid."

"I see there's no way out of it, and I shall have to tell you girls a story that will make you all scream and dream nightmares filled with revolvers and skulking figures and masked faces and lonely highways."

All of the thirteen members and the Guardian of Flamingo Camp Fire, Marion's mother, sister, and brother were present at this scene in the big living room of the Stanlock home. Mr.Stanlock covertly watched the faces of his auditors and was pleased to note that his bandying words were rapidly bringing the tension back to normal. Young Master Harold at this point helped his father's purpose along remarkably by piping forth:

"It's mighty funny if a man can't be out after dark without a lot o' women jumpin' on 'im."

Nobody with a grain of humor in his soul, if that is where the sense of fun is located, could have restrained a laugh at that remark. In a moment it would have been difficult for any one of those present to realize how tragically serious they had all been a few minutes before.

After the chorus of laughter had subsided, Mr.Stanlock sat down in a large upholstered armchair, and remarked to his unconsciously brilliant son:

"You are a great protector of women-oppressed man, aren't you, Harold. Your chief virtue along this line is your ability to get the philosophical high spots of every-day gossip. But don't stop there, my able young advocate. Do you realize that your father has had no dinner and that this exacting bevy of girls is going to force me to suffer the pangs of hunger until I have told my story?"

"I just told Mary (the head maid) to get your dinner ready," Mrs.Stanlock interposed smilingly. "You won't need to go hungry more than fifteen minutes longer."

"I see that you don't appreciate an eager and attentive audience," Marion remarked, affecting to be deeply offended in behalf of her guests. "Very well, we'll wait until after you have satisfied a mere man's appetite, and then we'll condescend to listen."

"Oh, I can tell it in fifteen minutes while Mary is warming over the meat and potatoes. Now, get ready, all you young ladies, for the first shock. I was really and truly held up."

"Held up!" exclaimed several of the girls in chorus.

"Yes, held up, with guns pointed at the chauffeur's head by two masked men on a lonely highway."

"You're joking," said Marion, dubiously.

"All right," said the mine owner, settling back comfortably in his chair. "You insisted on my telling my story, and now that I have begun it, you won't believe my first sentence."

"Yes, I do believe it, papa," Marion said repentantly, going close to her father's chair and putting her arm around his neck. "I believe you were held up by two masked highwaymen with guns in a lonely spot, as you say. But how did you escape?"

"We were rescued by some boys!"

Although at the end of a sentence, Mr.Stanlock stopped so quickly that only a dull person could fail to notice it. His sudden stop, of course, was occasioned by the return to his mind of his promise to keep the secret of the Boy Scouts.

"Boys," said Mrs.Stanlock, wonderingly. "I didn't know that we had any heroes of that type in Hollyhill."

"They were some young fellows out hunting," explained the narrator. "They witnessed the hold-up and leveled their guns at the rascals and drove them away."

"Who are those boys?" Marion demanded, and one might almost have imagined from her manner that she had half a kingdom to bestow on the rescuers of her father.

"I'm afraid I can't give you their names," Mr.Stanlock replied slowly.

"You don't mean to say that you let them get away without finding out who they were, do you?" his daughter inquired with just a shade of indignation.

"No, not exactly that, for I can easily get all their names any time I want them. But I know also that they don't wish to get into the newspapers in connection with this affair."

"Can't you tell me who some of them are, papa?" Marion pleaded. "I want to know who it was that, perhaps, saved the life of my father."

"I can't tell you now, Marion. I have promised faithfully not to reveal their identity at present for very good reasons which they gave to me."

"Where is Jake, the driver, Henry?" asked Mrs.Stanlock. "I see you drove home alone."

"Jake proved himself to be a scoundrel and a traitor and when he discovered that I had found him out he vamoosed. I expect to swear out a warrant for his arrest tomorrow. Shortly before my usual time for coming home, I received a letter by messenger, supposedly from Mr. Mills, chairman of a special hospital committee that is looking after the sick members of striking miners' families. I had been expecting a call of a meeting and this letter stated that it was important that I be present. He lives out on the Foothill pike near the quarries. I thought that I would make a quick run out there and call you up from his home and let you know how late I would be. Well, I didn't get there. It seems that Jake was one of the conspirators in a plot to get me out there and waylay me. By the way, that makes me think I ought to call Mills up and find out if he did call a meeting. The notice was on his stationery and it is just possible that wasn't a fake."

In a few moments Mr.Stanlock was talking with Mills on the phone. The latter was astonished, declared that he had no idea of calling a meeting that night.

"Well, it's lucky I kept the notice," the mining president muttered. "That'll be something interesting to show to the police tomorrow."

CHAPTER X

MR STANLOCK AMUSED

"I understand now how a mathematician could write 'Alice in Wonderland'," Helen Nash remarked to Marion after Mr.Stanlock had withdrawn to the diningroom and his belated meal.

"How is that?" the hostess inquired, looking curiously at her friend.

"Why, your father, I suppose, has been thinking in terms of tons of coal all day—"

"Carloads," Marion corrected, with a toss of levity.

"Well, make it carloads," Helen assented. "That's better to my purpose, more like a multiplication table, instead of addition. But it must be about as dry as mathematics."

"Oh, I get you," Marion exclaimed delightedly. "You mean that it is quite as remarkable for a coal operator, with carloads of coal and soot weighing down his imagination all day, to come home in the evening and spin off a lot of nonsense like a comedian as it is for a mathematician to have written 'Alice's Adventures in Wonderland'."

"Precisely," answered Helen.

"Well, I don't know but you're right. Anyway, I wouldn't detract from such a nice compliment paid to the dearest daddy on earth. Still, after leaving the atmosphere of his carloads of coal he had experienced the diversion of being held up."

"By two masked men with guns on a lonely highway," supplemented Helen.

"Yes."

"And later found that his driver had turned traitor and planned to deliver him into the hands of the enemy."

"Yes."

"I don't see any diversion or inspiration in that sort of experience. Many a man would have come home in a very depressed state of mind after such an adventure. And yet he came home, found everybody scared to death, and before he even began his story had us all laughing just as Alice would at some of the contortions behind the looking glass. And he kept us smiling even when he told of the masked would-be kidnappers standing in the middle of the road and pointing pistols at the driver of his automobile."

"Kidnappers," repeated Marion in puzzled surprise. "Why do you say kidnappers?"

The two girls were alone in the library when this conversation took place. All of the other guests, feeling that the members of the family would prefer to be left alone following the startling occurrences of the evening, had withdrawn to their rooms. Helen was about to bid her friend good-night when her remark regarding Mr.Stanlock's happy personal faculties opened the discussion as here recorded. She hesitated a few moments before answering the last inquiry; then she said:

"Don't you think that those men intended to kidnap your father? What other explanation can you find for their actions?"

"I hadn't tried to figure out their motive," Marion replied thoughtfully. "Father called it a hold-up and I took his word for it."

"But he had no money with him, did he?"

"No, I think not. He seldom carries much money."

"And it is hardly reasonable to suppose that this plot between the chauffeur and the two highwaymen was for the purpose of murder. They would have gone about it in some other way. This one leaves too many traces behind."

"Yes," Marion admitted.

"Well, the only reasonable conclusion you can reach with the robbery and murder motives out of the way, is that the plotters wished to take your father prisoner and hold him some place until they got what they wanted."

"But what did they want?" asked the bewildered Marion.

"That's for your father to suspect and the police to find out," said Helen shrewdly. "Personally, I haven't a doubt that the strike has everything to do with it."

"What makes you think so?"

"The threatening letter that you received at the Institute. Show that to your father tonight and suggest that he turn it over to the police."

"I will," Marion promised. "In this new excitement I forgot all about it. I didn't even show it to mother. Just as soon as papa finishes his dinner, I'm going to show that letter to him. I'll go upstairs now and get it. You wait here and be present when we talk it over, Helen. You're so good at offering suggestions that maybe with you present we can all work out some kind of solution of what has been going on."

Marion hastened up to her room and returned presently with both of the anonymous letters she had received in Westmoreland. A few minutes later her father and mother both entered the library with the evident purpose in mind of holding a lengthy conference on the problems growing out of Mr.Stanlock's business troubles.

"Papa, do you think those men tried to kidnap you?" Marion inquired by way of introducing the subject.

Mr.Stanlock laughed heartily.

"Kidnap me!" he exclaimed. "Well, that's a good one. I thought they only kidnapped kids."

"Father," the girl pleaded; "do be serious with me. I've got something very important to show you, something I forgot all about until Helen reminded me. Helen thinks those men tried to kidnap you, and she's a pretty wise girl, as I've had occasion to find out."

"If Helen said that, she surely must be a wise girl or else she has made a pretty accurate guess," was the mine owner's reply.

"Then they did want to kidnap you?"

"Absolutely no doubt of it. They've got some kind of retreat in the mountains, and planned to carry me off there and keep me prisoner."

"What for?"

"Why, to force me to yield to some of their demands, which are utterly impossible and unreasonable. First, they demand an increase of wages that would force us into a receivership sooner or later and again they demand the adoption of a cooperative plan which eventually would make them owners of the mines, if there were any possibility of it working, and there isn't. It's a most ridiculous hold-up, the responsibility for which rests with a few fanatical leaders of doubtful integrity."

"What do you think of these letters?" Marion asked, handing the two anonymous missives to her father. "I received them by mail at the Institute last night, but neglected to read them until we were all on the train this morning."

As Mr.Stanlock read them, his brow contracted sternly. He could treat lightly any hostile attack on himself, but when danger threatened members of his family or their intimate friends, all signs of levity disappeared from his manner and he was ready at once to meet with all his energy the source of the danger, whether it be human or an element of inanimate nature.

"This" he said, as he finished reading and held up the letter signed with a skull and cross-bones, "undoubtedly came from the source where the plot to kidnap me originated. They are pretty well organized and determined to go the limit. Of course, you girls must give up your plans to work among the strikers' families. It would be foolhardy and probably would result in somebody's getting hurt."

"How about the other letter?" Marion asked.

"I don't know," was the reply. "It doesn't seem to amount to much. I hardly think it is to be taken as a threat. Have you no idea who sent it?"

"Some of the girls think it was sent by some of the Boy Scouts at Spring Lake. You see they came up in full force to Hiawatha on the night when we held our Grand Council Fire. It was a complete surprise on us, exceedingly well done and about as clever as you could expect from the cleverest boys. Before they left, several of them boasted openly that they were planning another surprise for some of us, and they dared us to find out in advance what it was."

"No doubt that is what this note means," Mr.Stanlock declared so positively and such a gleam of interest in his eyes that Marion could not help wondering just a little.

"What makes you so certain about it?" she inquired. "I don't see any real proof in those words as to what they mean or who wrote them."

"No, no, of course not," agreed Mr.Stanlock with seemingly uncalled for glibness; "but then, you see, it is more reasonable to suspect that this note came from the boys than from the strikers. If it is between the two,—the boys and the strikers,—I say forget the strikers and be sure that the boys sent this note."

"I wish that the boys would spring their surprise tonight and settle the question of that note," said Marion.

"Why?" inquired her father with the faint light of a smile in his eyes.

"Because I don't like the uncertainty of the thing. Uncertainty always bothers me, and this is a more than ordinary case."

"But how could the boys spring their surprise without coming to Hollyhill?" her father asked.

"That's just it," she returned with a quick glance of suspicion toward both her father and her mother. "Do you know, I found myself wondering several times if Clifford wouldn't bring some of those boys down here some time during the holidays."

Mr.Stanlock laughed, but he would have given a good deal to be able to recall the noise he made. It was really a noise, as he must have admitted himself, and so hollow as to indicate something decidedly unlike spontaneous amusement.

Marion caught herself in a brown study several times over these circumstances and her father's manner before she went to sleep that night.

CHAPTER XI

A MAN OF BIG HEART AND QUEER NOTIONS

Christmas was a big event at Hollyhill. Hollyhill was well named. Perhaps some old patriarch a century or two back conceived the inspiration of the name while playing Santa Claus with the little tots of the household and pretending to have slid down the chimney without getting a speck of soot on his bulging vestments.

Perhaps he imagined, while mother woke the children and had them peek through a "crack in the door" at the white whiskered visitor stuffing their stockings full of presents, that he had tethered his prancing team of reindeer to a holly tree outside. Certainly there seemed to have been material for such imagination, for tradition said that the hill on which the first houses of the first settlement were built had at one time been richly adorned with a species of American Ilex, and even now there remained here and there carefully preserved remnants of that reported original wealth of the wilderness.

Whether or not this conjectural history of the settlement had anything to do with the cheerful mid-winter holiday developments of the community need not be argued at length. An argument would render the truth flat and insipid if it should prove to be in accord with poetic tradition. So what's the use?

In mid-winter everybody just knew that Hollyhill as a child had been nursed in the snow trimmed evergreen lap of Christmas. Not that this municipality had a corner on mid-winter holiday generosity to the exclusion of all other communities. The chief outstanding fact in this relation was that the inhabitants, or those so fortunate as to be in a position to give and receive abundantly, believed Hollyhill to be the most generous Christmas town on earth, and there was nobody sufficiently interested to make a denial and follow it up with proof.

Much of the credit for this condition was due to the leading man of the place, Richard P. Stanlock, president and controlling power of the Hollyhill Coal Mining company, which owned a string of mines in the mountain district near the divisional line of two states. Besides being the leading citizen, Mr.Stanlock was the "biggest" man in town, because of the position to which he had risen, his ability to hold it, and the influence that went with it. What he said usually went, but his hand was not always evident. He liked to see things done, doubtless enjoyed the realization that his was the great moving power that produced results, but didn't give a fig to have anybody else know it. To his intimate friends, who were few, and to the many with whom he would pass the time of day, he was as common in word and manner as the average householder with nothing more pretentious in life than the earning of his daily bread.

But in spite of all this simplicity and personal retirement Mr.Stanlock was a good deal of a mystery to many citizens who knew really little about him. Or perhaps he was a mystery to these fellow townsfolk because of his modest qualities. Knowing little about him, they imagined more. Leading citizens who knew his good qualities were ever ready with a word of praise for him. But the trouble was, the needed tangible evidence of his broad philanthropy was utterly lacking. Seldom was there a visible connecting link between him and a good deed. And so the praise of his work in pulpit, press and other public and semi-public places fell as platitudes before a considerable number of skeptics, whose favorite reply to this sort of thing was something like—

"Bunk."

But Marion knew that it wasn't "bunk." She was one of the few confidants that gained an intimate understanding of the wealthy mine owner's character. She knew that he was the secret financial backer of an organization of settlement workers which kept close watch on the needs of the miners and their families, many of whom were so woefully ignorant that about the only way to handle them was by appealing to their appetites, their sympathies and their prejudices. She knew, too, that he had strong connections constantly at work fostering and promoting the best of activities for advancement of the civic welfare, that Christmas was one of his secret hobbies and that it was practically impossible for this city of 40,000 inhabitants to neglect this opportunity for a revival of good fellowship and good cheer so long as her father had his hand on the electric key of public generosity.

Christmas was a blaze of glory every year in Hollyhill. Public halls, churches, and theaters were the scenes of the liveliest activities for several days and nights before and after this biggest event of the winter season. Nor was the celebration confined to the more prosperous sections of the town, but extended into the heart of the mining settlement, where Christmas tinsel and lights were lavished without consideration of cost and nobody was allowed to pass the season without being impressively reminded as to just what turkey roast and cranberry sauce tasted like.

So skilfully were these programs put into effect that seldom was a hint dropped from any source that Richard Perry Stanlock was entitled to the slightest credit for these magnificent doings. He spent Christmas at home in a quiet unassuming way amid the family decorations of holly and mistletoe, and a vast litter of presents, oranges, apples, nuts, and candy.

Marion knew that her father's greatest vanity was his secret pride in his ability to put over the biggest generosity of the year without its being traceable to him. One day a girl acquaintance of her asked her if she knew that her father spent $25,000 every year for Christmas. Marion laughed; later she laughingly reported the query to Mr.Stanlock. Next day this girl friend's uncle, one of the philanthropist's agents, was called in on the carpet and given a lecture on the wisdom of guarding his remarks such as he had never before dreamed of receiving.

"Papa," the millionaire's older daughter said to him one day; "don't you think it is foolish to keep secret all these generous things that you are doing?"

"Why do you think it is foolish, my dear?" he replied with an expression of shrewd amusement. He was certain that she would have difficulty in answering his question.

"Well," she began slowly, then admitted: "I don't know."

"I'm very glad you don't know," said her father with evident satisfaction. "If you had tried to give a reason, I should have been greatly disappointed. No explanation of that suggestion could be based on anything but family pride, which is one form of vanity."

"No," Marion differed thoughtfully. "There is one explanation based on human caution and wisdom. I am afraid that you are misunderstood by the very people whose confidence you should seek to cultivate, that is the miners. Some of them don't like you very well. They think that you personally are a hard taskmaster and that the attentions and relief which really come from you in times of need, are bestowed on them by persons who feel that they have to help them because of your failure to do the right thing by them. Why don't you, papa, go right among them and tell them that you are going to do everything you can for them, raise their wages, maybe, and make them love you personally?"

"It isn't my nature, Marion, to do it that way," Mr.Stanlock replied. "There is nothing in the world that would be so distasteful to me as assuming the role of a philanthropist or a hero. It spoils every man to some extent who tries it.

Personal vanity is the greatest enemy that man has to guard against. I've guarded myself against it thus far successfully, I think, and I'm not going to let it get me in the future if I can help it."

Marion felt like saying that her father's fear of vanity might some day get him into trouble with his men, but she refrained from so expressing herself. On the occasion before us she recalled that conversation, for she realized that the strike was a result, in part, of the very misunderstanding that she had anticipated. Several clever leaders among the miners had spread the report about that Mr.Stanlock had become immensely wealthy by overworking and underpaying his men, while he caused to be circulated through various channels numerous undetailed reports of his generosity, philanthropy and public spirit.

When she invited the members of Flamingo Camp Fire to be her guests and work with her among the poor and hunger-suffering families of the strikers she did not realize the seriousness of the situation with reference to the feeling of the miners toward her father. Now she felt that the condition of affairs was more than she could cope with and from the day of her arrival home she was constantly in fear lest some dread catastrophe should befall the family because the "biggest man" in Hollyhill kept himself severely fortified against the adulation of his fellow townsmen and the character weakening influence of personal vanity.

CHAPTER XII

A MYSTERIOUS DISAPPEARANCE

The Flamingo Camp Fire arrived at the Stanlock home on Friday. Christmas was scheduled on the calendar to fall on the following Wednesday.

From the day of their arrival all of the girls were busy with Christmas preparations. Every one of them, several weeks before, had taken on her the task of making, buying, or assembling from parts purchased a score or more of presents. As one of the chief aims of Hiawatha Institute was to teach wealthy men's daughters how to be economical, it goes without saying that each of these girls had on hand no enviable Winter Task.

Madame Cleaver laid the matter very plainly before her two hundred and forty-odd girls. She had observed that the Christmas problem had a tendency to make some of the students of her school sympathize with Old Scrooge. If Christmas wasn't a humbug it could very easily be made a nuisance.

Madame Cleaver agreed with them in this respect. She told them so. Furthermore, she added:

"I don't wish you to understand that there is anything compulsory in the giving of presents on such occasions. One of the dangers of this sort of thing is that it is likely to become a perfunctory affair with thousands taking part because they feel they have to. Also Christmas is exploited by many people. Their sympathy for the good-fellowship of the occasion is measured largely by the dollars and cents that it pours into their coffers.

"You should see all these drawbacks and then decide for yourselves whether the advantages of Christmas overbalance the drawbacks. For my part I believe that they do and I enjoy the day and the season. But don't take my word for it. Decide for yourselves."

The result was that everybody at the Institute got busy several weeks before the holiday season, and the manner in which the products of girl ingenuity began to pile up must have been satisfying indeed to the head of the school. But the work was not all done when the Camp Fire arrived at Hollyhill, most of the girls still having enough to do to keep them busy almost up to Christmas eve.

Mr.Stanlock advised the girls not to leave the house under any consideration after night, and engaged three detectives, who were given instructions to follow and protect any of Marion's guests who might desire to go shopping or make other journeys about the city in the day time. Automobiles, with drivers, were within ready call for these men at any time. It was understood, also, that no journeys were to be made into the section of the city inhabited by the miners and their families.

Thus far the strike had not been attended by violence of any sort or the destruction of property. The men had simply ceased to work and had submitted their demands to the president of the company. The latter realized at once that the employees were being led by an unusual type of labor agitators, who might be expected to employ unusual methods to gain their ends. The man who appeared to be the leader was as unusual in appearance as he was in methods pursued. He was about thirty-five years old, but looked five or eight years younger. He had first been employed in the mines about six months before as an operator of an electric chain-cutter machine, but he had not long been connected with the work before his influence among the men began to be felt. To the casual observer, he was a quiet sharp-eyed man, who seldom spoke, under ordinary circumstances, unless he was first spoken to. But he got in communication with all his fellow workers in some mysterious manner and before long, in spite of the fact that he was not what is popularly known as a "mixer," everybody from shovelers to machine men knew him as Dave, the chain-cutter man. He had the reputation of being able to do "half again as much work as any man in the slope." Although Mr.Stanlock knew of the influence of this man on the miners almost from the day when the strike was called, the only name by which he heard him spoken of during almost the entire period of the tie-up was "Dave, the chain-cutter man."

Little of special interest relative to the strike, so far as the girls were concerned, took place on the last Saturday and Sunday before Christmas. Mr.Stanlock reported the recent occurrences to the police in detail, but what the police planned to do was not communicated in the form of hint or suggestion to the members of Flamingo Fire. If Mr.Stanlock knew, he kept the information a close secret. In harmony with his habitual reticence on business matters, he sought to avoid further discussion of the subject.

On Saturday, however, there was added to the events of the season one item of great importance, which would have caused Marion no little uneasiness could she have caught more than the most superficial hint concerning it. This hint was so superficial that it consisted merely of a glimpse at the address and postmark on a letter that arrived at the house with the early mail. Marion took the letters and papers from the mail box, and as she was distributing them she observed the Hollyhill postmark on an envelope addressed in a man's handwriting to Helen Nash.

"I wonder who it can be," the hostess mused as she laid the letter on Helen's dresser. "I didn't know that she was on specially friendly terms with any of the boys of Hollyhill. But then you can never know what to expect of her. You find out what she is going to do when she does it."

In spite of the paradox, no truer statement of Helen's nature had ever been made. She said nothing to any of the girls about the letter she had received and if subsequent events had not recalled the incident, Marion probably would have forgotten it entirely.

The three detectives employed by Mr.Stanlock were housed in the now vacant sleeping quarters of the chauffeur over the garage. A buzzer connected with the house and an agreed signal system of "1," "2," "3" served as a means of quick information as to how many of the men were wanted at any given time. Sunday morning another chauffeur, engaged by Mr.Stanlock, arrived and was housed with the detectives.

It was not the duty of the latter, of course, to accompany or follow anybody leaving the house unless they were called. Hence it was quite possible for any of the guests to start out alone and make a trip to any part of the city without the protection of a watchful guard. The possibility that any of the guests might desire to take such a course did not occur to Marion or any other member of the household. It was presumed that everybody would gladly accept such protection on every occasion when it seemed advisable.

As a matter of fact, however, the detectives had little to do on Saturday and Sunday. Only three of the girls made shopping trips on Saturday and all took an automobile ride Sunday afternoon. This was the sum total of their activities away from the Stanlock home, with the exception of one instance, of which there was no hint until late in the afternoon.

About six o'clock Marion suddenly became mindful of the fact that she had not seen Helen since their return from the automobile drive three hours earlier, and she began a search for her. She first went upstairs to her room to see if her friend were there. Probably she was tired and had lain down to rest and fallen asleep. But an inspection of the room failed to discover Helen.

Considerably puzzled, Marion now hunted up every other person in the house and inquired for the missing girl. Not one of them remembered seeing her since the return from the drive. The girl hostess was now thoroughly alarmed and her fears were speedily communicated to the others. Everybody joined in the search and every nook and corner capable of concealing a human form was examined.

Helen Nash was not in the house and there seemed to be no reasonable explanation of her disappearance.

CHAPTER XIII

"FIND HER, OR I'LL FIND HER MYSELF"

Mr.Stanlock came home from a meeting of mining stockholders about the time when consternation over the disappearance of Helen was at its height. After the particulars of the affair, so far as they were known, had been explained to him, he asked:

"Where are the detectives?"

The question fell with something of a shock on the ears of the assembled searchers who had just completed a second fruitless hunt through the house. Why had they not thought of the trio of "mystery masters" before?

"We ought to have called them in at once," Mrs.Stanlock said. "I suppose they've gone by this time, but I'll see."

She pushed the buzzer button in the hall and soon the new chauffeur appeared at the side entrance. Yes, the detectives had gone, but he knew where they could be found—at the High Peak Athletic Club.

Mr.Stanlock at once called up the club and soon had one of the detectives on the wire.

"Can you men come over at once?" he inquired. "One of the girls has disappeared and we are afraid that something serious has happened."

"Yes, we'll be there right away," was the answer.

Twenty minutes later there was a ring at the door and the three detectives, a tall thin man, a short heavy man, and a squarely built angular man, were ushered in.

The short heavy man, named Meyers, was the most talkative of the three. He put forth a string of questions as to when and where Helen was last seen and what she was doing. Had anybody seen her go out of the house? Nobody had. Was there anything peculiar in her manner in the course of the day? Nothing peculiar. What kind of a girl was she? What were her most noticeable characteristics? Had she any pronounced likes and dislikes? Was she in the habit of doing things just to be contrary? Was she a girl of good judgment, or flighty and light-headed?

58

These questions brought out nothing of tangible advantage, and No. 1 rested apparently well satisfied with the keenness of his record thus far made. No. 2 now took up the inquiry. He was the squarely built angular fellow with deep-set eyes, quiet demeanor and few words. His first question was:

"Has Miss Nash any other friends living in Hollyhill?"

"No, I think not," Marion replied; "no particular friends."

"None that she ever corresponds with?" persisted the man with the deep-set eyes.

Marion started visibly. Sudden recollection of the letter received by Helen the day before came to her.

"She got a letter postmarked Hollyhill yesterday," the young hostess replied.

"Who was it from?"

"I don't know. I didn't know that she was corresponding with anybody in the town. But the address on the envelope looked as if it was written by a man."

"Do you suppose you could find that letter?"

"I'll go upstairs and look," Marion said, suiting the action to the word.

In a few minutes she returned with a waste paper basket in her hands.

"Helen was sharing my room with me," she said. "A letter has been torn up and thrown in the basket. As I didn't do it, it must be Helen's."

"This begins to look like something," the tall man said with a nod of approval, picking up several bits of paper from the basket. "She's torn it up in pretty small pieces, but if we all get busy we ought to be able to put them together in a short time."

"Let's go out to the dining room table," Mrs.Stanlock proposed, leading the way as she spoke.

In a few moments all were seated around the large fumed oak table from which the spread had been removed as the hard wood surface was much better for the task of piecing the letter together.

It was, indeed, a tedious task, but with so many working together progress was fairly rapid. Within fifteen minutes half a dozen sentence sections of several words each had been joined in their phrase order. These were soon followed by three or four more and presently one of the girls found a connecting link between two sections thus forming a complete sentence. Imagine the thrill that went through everyone as Mr.Stanlock read the following:

"Get your friends out of Hollyhill as soon as possible."

"I bet this letter was written by the same person who wrote the skull-and-cross-bones letter to me," Marion ventured confidently.

"That's the very idea that just occurred to me," Miss Ladd declared as she fitted "no" and "difference" together and then tried to find a connecting edge on the pieces held by her neighbor to the left.

Fortunately the letter had been written on only one side of a large sheet of paper, so that they could be pasted in correlative positions on another sheet provided for the purpose.

Finally the patchwork was completed, in so far as the material at hand made completeness possible. A few of the bits of torn paper were missing, so that a word was wanting here and there in the text, but apparently the idea and purpose of the writer did not suffer from these vacancies. The letter as read at last by Mr.Stanlock was as follows:

"Dear ...r

"You have failed to do what I ... you to do. I told you that it was ... dangerous to bring the girls here. The letter of warning to Miss Stan ... did no good.... I want to warn you again and ... ... last time. Get your friends out of Hollyhill as soon as possible. I won't be responsible for what occurs. It makes no difference if you have given up your original purpose. Some of the men are so worked up that they are liable to do almost anything. If you can't get the rest out of town go yourself, or you may get hurt.

"D...."

"Ah, ha!" exclaimed the short, heavy and loquacious detective, "That explains the whole thing. Miss Nash has gone out of town."

"She hasn't done any such thing," Marion exclaimed indignantly, springing to her feet. "Helen isn't that kind of a girl. I know she is peculiar, but she isn't a coward. It's evident now that she knew something about affairs here that resulted in the sending of that threatening letter to me, and she kept her information secret for some reason. Whatever her reason was, she meant all right."

"Did she at any time urge or suggest that it would not be well for the girls to come here in the holidays?" Mr.Stanlock inquired.

"Never a word," Marion replied, positively. "I admit that once or twice I noticed that there was something peculiar in her manner, and it may have had something to do with her condition back of these developments, but that is all."

"How do you account for her disappearance?" asked Detective Meyer, with puzzled humility.

"I don't pretend to account for it," Marion replied, quickly. "That's a problem for you men to solve. All I know is that Helen did not intentionally desert us. She's gone, and she went for some reason, and I believe that reason is connected with the letter. Now, it's up to you men to find her, and, if you don't find her pretty quick, I'll go and find her myself."

A murmur of applause swept the room.

"We'll do it," declared the tall, thin detective.

"If it's within human power," conditioned the square-built, deep-eyed man.

The talkative gentleman of genius said nothing. All three of them left the house a few minutes later.

CHAPTER XIV

TRAPPED

There was little sleep for anyone at the Stanlock home that night. The mystery of the patched-up letter, coupled with Helen's apparently voluntary disappearance and the fear that she had been led into a trap of some sort, in line with the threat contained in the skull-and-cross-bones letter, kept everybody up until long after midnight. Meanwhile, Mr.Stanlock called up the police station and asked the lieutenant in charge to come over and begin work on a new angle of the strike developments.

"One of the girls has disappeared, and we are afraid that something serious has happened," he told the officer over the telephone.

The latter soon drove up to the house in an automobile and was admitted by Mr.Stanlock. The conference lasted half an hour, but before half this time had elapsed Lieut. Larkin had the station on the wire and was giving instructions to the desk sergeant.

To add to the difficulty of the problem, snow began to fall about 5 o'clock, and developed almost into a blizzard in three or four hours.

Next morning the two newspapers of Hollyhill carried big headlines and column-and-a-half stories of the new strike development, suggestive of a far-reaching plot that might result in tragedy. Mr.Stanlock had during the evening received all newspaper calls over a special wire in his private room, so as not to disturb the guests with the publicity end of the affair.

In the afternoon Mrs.Stanlock announced that she, being an officer of the woman's club with an important duty to perform, must attend a committee meeting from 3 until 4:30 o'clock, and she asked Miss Ladd to accompany her. The latter consented, but cautioned the girls against leaving the house, inasmuch as the three detectives were no longer available for guard duty, having been directed to devote their entire time to the search for Helen.

There were now at the house only the twelve remaining Camp Fire Girls and the kitchen maid, Kitty Koepke.

Marion's younger sister and brother were attending a children's afternoon party a few blocks away. The new chauffeur had been summoned by Mrs.Stanlock to take her and Miss Ladd to the club rooms where the committee meeting was to be held.

About 3 o'clock a newspaper photographer and a reporter arrived. The girls allowed a group picture to be taken and the reporter was granted an interview.

Half an hour after the newspaper men departed, there came a ring at the front door. As Mary, the head servant, was out, Marion answered the ring and found at the entrance a woman of middle age, dressed in plain black, who spoke to her, in quick, eager accents, thus:

"Is this Miss Marion Stanlock?"

"It is," the girl answered.

"I am Mrs. Eddy, who moved into one of those vacant houses two blocks from here," the woman explained. "I have some information of interest to you."

"Is it about Helen Nash?" Marion asked, so eagerly that there could be no mistaking the subject nearest her heart.

The woman nodded and smiled, and Marion seized her by the arm and almost dragged her into the hall and thence into the reception room.

"Where is she?—tell me quickly!" Two of the other girls in the drawing-room, hearing these words and surmising their significance, came rushing in and caught the visitor's answer, thus:

"She's over at my house. She came there last night. I had no idea who she was until I saw the articles in the newspaper—I didn't get it until late—and then I came right over."

"But," said Marion, apprehensively, "why didn't she come right home? What was the matter—couldn't she explain who she was?"

"The girl was not in her right mind," Mrs. Eddy said. "She was in a delirium. It was about 10 o'clock at night, and evidently she had been tramping the streets for hours in the storm."

"How is she now? Oh! I must go right to her! Did she get lost in the storm? Girls, girls! Come here! Helen's found! Is she—is she—ill—very ill, Mrs. Eddy?"

"I don't think she is seriously ill," the woman replied, with an expression of sweet encouragement. "I had a doctor call, and he didn't seem to think there was any immediate danger, although she hasn't talked rationally yet. She is in bed, and has considerable fever."

"Would it be all right for me to go and see her—is it against the doctor's orders? I'd be very careful; and, besides, I'm a nurse—in fact, we all are nurses."

"Oh, to be sure—it will be all right for you to come—all of you may come if you wish. You can go in one at a time, quietly. Then a couple of you may remain and help nurse her. I really need help, for I am all alone, and sat up all night with her, and have been close to her most of the day. Perhaps it would be well for you girls to make arrangements for relief nursing watches. You are perfectly welcome to keep her at my home until she is well, if you will relieve me of the necessity of nursing her."

"Come on, girls; get your wraps; we will all go over. It's only a couple of blocks. Hurry, everybody!"

"Wait, and I'll tell Kitty we're going out," Marion said.

She ran through several rooms, calling "Kittie! Kittie!" but received no response.

"I wonder where she is," the hostess said, in a puzzled manner. "Well, we haven't time to find her. Come on."

"I think I saw her go out more than half an hour ago," Harriet Newcomb said. "She called someone up on the telephone, and then put her hat and coat on and went out the side way, and I haven't seen her since."

"That's strange," Marion commented. Then the subject was forgotten. The twelve girls and their leader were walking rapidly toward the place where Mrs. Eddy, the good Samaritan, had taken in and cared for the girl whom every one of them loved as they would have loved a sister.

The house they stopped in front of was rather dingy and forbidding. It was a large brick structure, set back a hundred feet from the street on a plot of ground nearly an acre in extent. Most of the windows were darkened with green blinds two generations out of date.

Mrs. Eddy put a key into the lock and opened the door. Then she stepped aside and motioned the girls to enter, and they did so as if moved by a spell that they were unable to resist. Then the woman herself entered, closed the door and put the key into the lock and turned it. If the twelve Camp Fire

Girls had no suspicions as to the genuineness of the motives of the woman up to this time, they had good and sufficient reason to anticipate something dreadful when they saw her take the key from the lock and put it in her coat pocket.

And still if there were any doubts in their minds after this act, they were effectively dispelled by the sound of a man's voice coming through a doorway from a dimly lighted room to the right, speaking thus:

"Now, young ladies, let me warn you to be quiet. You have been led into a trap; but you will not be hurt in any way if you obey orders. One scream from any of you will be followed by a blow with a club that will silence you for a long time—maybe, forever. This way, please. Everybody be quiet and sensible, and you will be well treated."

CHAPTER XV

A PILE OF SCRAP LUMBER

Conditions and developments seemed to work favorably for the mysterious trappers of the Camp Fire Girls. In the first place, when Mrs.Stanlock returned home and found the house without an occupant, except KittieKoepke, who was working away very quietly in the kitchen, it was difficult for her to suspect anything wrong.

"Where are the girls, Kittie?" she inquired, and the other replied, with a suggestion of foreign accent:

"Oh, they just gone out for a walk. They be back soon, I guess."

"I hope they didn't go far," Mrs.Stanlock said, concernedly. "They ought to be very careful. It will be getting dark before very long. It's cloudy and looks like more snow. How long have they been gone?"

"About half an hour," Kittie answered. "I went out to the drug store to get something for my toothache, and when I came back they was gone."

This was the first reference that Mrs.Stanlock heard regarding Kittie's toothache, but she accepted the statement for its face value and waited hopefully for an early return of her daughter and her daughter's guests. Half an hour went by and the girls did not appear. Darkness was now visibly gathering. Mrs.Stanlock was becoming uneasy and called up her husband's office, but Mr.Stanlock had already started for home. By the time he arrived, the good woman was almost prostrated, so rapidly were fear and apprehension taking possession of her.

The big coal operator scented danger at once. Immediately after gathering the principal details of the day's occurrences, he got the police station on the wire and communicated them to the officer in charge.

Drastic measures were resorted to at once. The day shift of uniformed and ununiformed guardians of the law was summoned back to duty, and a posse of available citizens were sworn in.

About 7 o'clock a posse of citizen policemen, led by three or four uniformed members of the regular force, began a canvass of the neighborhood to discover information that might suggest a clew as to the whereabouts of the missing girls. Half an hour later a woman informed one of the canvassers that she had seen eight or ten girls enter the yard of the old Buckholz place

66

between 3 and 4 o'clock, but had not noticed whether they went into the house or not. The man to whom this statement was made blew a whistle as an agreed signal to the other searchers that he had important information and soon a score of them were running toward him from all directions.

A comparison of notes disclosed the fact that another member of the party of canvassers had received a similar statement from another resident in the neighborhood. It was decided, therefore, to delay no further but to proceed at once to the house in question, while one of the men hastened to Mr.Stanlock with news of developments in order that he might be present and direct the next move.

The latter was waiting at home, ready to answer a telephone or personal call from any of the central points of investigation. The nervous strain of the apparent certainty, by this time, that the disappearance of Marion and her guests portended serious developments had compelled Mrs.Stanlock to take to her bed and summon a physician and a nurse. The call from the searchers in the neighborhood took Mr.Stanlock from her bedside, and so speedily did he respond to it that he was at the entrance of the Buckholz house almost as soon as the party of citizens and uniformed policemen.

"Don't hesitate, men," he urged. "I know the owner of this house very well and will take all responsibility for damages on my own shoulders. If the door won't give, break it down."

"Maybe there is somebody at home," Lieutenant Larkin suggested. "Let's ring the bell first"

"Well, come on," said Mr.Stanlock. "We'll soon find out if there's anyone in the house."

He led the way up the weather-beaten but fairly well preserved steps and pulled the knob of the old fashioned doorbell. Then they waited expectantly, straining their ears to catch the sound of the approach of someone within. But no such sound reached them.

It appearing evident now that the house was temporarily without an inmate, the searchers for the thirteen mysteriously vanished girls decided to force their way in. Under ordinary conditions, this act would have been recognized as burglary, but the present circumstances were so extraordinary that legal consequences had no terrors for any of those present. Accordingly an examination was made of the two first story windows, two of which were found unlocked. With the aid of a box discovered under the rear porch, several of the men climbed in one by one and found themselves in a large unfurnished room, architecturally intended, perhaps, as a dining room. Each of the three uniformed policemen carried an electric flashlight and with the aid of these an examination of the house was begun.

But not a trace of the missing girls could be found.

"What next?" one of the men asked.

"The basement," suggested Lieut. Larkin.

Mr.Stanlock opened the door at the head of the stairway and flashed his light down the steps.

"Wait a minute," he said, barring the entrance. "Let's examine the ground as we go. These steps have dust on them, and there are shoe prints in the dust, and, yes, sir, as sure as you are alive, they are the prints of women's shoes, and there are a lot of 'em, unless I'm mistaken. Be careful now, men. Follow me single file and come down along the left side of the stairway as close the wall as possible so as not to spoil those footprints in the dust."

"Look out," said Mr.Stanlock. "There may be some desperate characters down there with guns. Better let me go first—I have most at stake."

"Not much!" replied the lieutenant. "We'll never win the European war without charging the trenches. All I ask is that you get the fellow that gets me. So here goes."

Cautiously he descended the stairs, followed by the five men who had entered the house with him. But their anticipations were groundless. Not a sign of human life did they find in the large, square, deep basement, or cellar, more properly.

Some of the men looked puzzled, Mr.Stanlock was evidently laboring under increasing distress, but Lieut Larkin's curiosity seemed to grow.

"Some queer stories have been told about this place," he said; "and I'm wondering if now is not the time to put them to a test. They are pretty wild stories, almost as wild as haunted house yarns, but there may be thing to them."

"I've heard something about them myself," said Mr.Stanlock. "You refer to the stories about the building of this house over an old mine, I suppose?

This cellar was said to have been the mouth of the shaft of the mine enlarged."

"That's it," the lieutenant replied. "Now, let's look about and see if there is anything to it."

He began to flash his light over the floor, walls, and contents of the cellar. The latter consisted principally of barrels, boxes and a nondescript pile of scrap lumber. Most of this was heaped against the south wall.

Presently something in the pile of lumber held the attention of the lieutenant, who began to examine it more closely.

"Look here," he said, addressing Mr.Stanlock. "Do you see any difference between this pile of lumber and that dry goods box over there?"

"I was just noticing that there was a heavy covering of dust on the box and little or none on the top pieces of lumber," the mine owner answered.

"That's just it," continued Lieut. Larkin, "and it can mean only one thing, that this pile of lumber has been moved recently. Now, the question, in view of the fact that the missing girls were seen entering this place today and in view of the shoe prints on the cellar stairway and the fact that they are not in the basement now is, Why?"

"The best way to find out is to move it again," suggested Sergeant Higgins.

"Exactly," agreed his superior officer. "Now, Johnson, you go upstairs and inform the other men what we are doing. We don't want them down here, for there's nothing they can do. Moreover, we don't want any more traveling up and down those steps than is absolutely necessary. Be careful, Johnson, on your way up."

"Excuse me, lieutenant," interposed Mr.Stanlock in a weak voice that bespoke the distress under which he was laboring. "I think I won't remain down here just now. I'll go up and carry that message to the men, if you wish. Let me know as soon as you can what you find."

CHAPTER XVI

HELEN AND THE STRIKE LEADER'S WIFE

But what had become of Helen Nash?

It was a very determined little woman who stole out of the Stanlock residence, with the contents of the last threatening letter fresh in her memory, after the return of the members of Flamingo Camp Fire from their Sunday afternoon drive. She walked briskly four blocks east and boarded a street car.

A twenty-minutes' ride took her into the heart of the mining tenement district. Reference to an address memorandum on a slip of paper that she carried in her handbag and a question to the conductor determined where she should get off.

Heaver street, the conductor told her, was three blocks east. With no evidence of a slackening of resolution, she proceeded as directed and was soon searching a long row of cottages, built along almost identical lines, for number 632.

Reaching this number, she ascended a flight of seven or eight steps and gave a quick turn to the old-fashioned fifteen-or-twenty-cent trip-action door bell. A pale-faced, care-worn woman of about 30 years, who might have been mistaken for 40, answered the ring. At sight of the caller she exclaimed in a voice that echoed years of toil and suffering:

"Helen!"

"Nell," was the greeting returned by the caller.

The woman stepped aside, and Helen stepped into a hall, whose sole furnishing consisted of a rag rug on the floor and a cheap hall-tree with a cracked mirror. Evidently it was the chief wardrobe of the house, for upon the twenty or more nails driven into the walls in fairly regular order were articles of both men's and women's wear, most of them bearing evidence of contact with hard labor. From the hall, Helen was conducted into the "front room," the only name it was ever known by, which communicated with the dining room through a cased opening without portieres. These two rooms were about as barely furnished as possible under a minimum of necessary articles and quality. A threadbare ingrain carpet covered the floor of the front room. A few rag rugs hid probably some of the worst gaps in the matching of the yellow-pine floor of the dining room.

As for human life in this house of pinch and poverty, it was hardly vigorous enough to attract attention ahead of the furnishings. Clinging to the faded skirts of their mother were three hungry-eyed anaemic children, a girl and two boys.

"How are you, Nell?" inquired Helen, giving the woman a kiss that seemed almost to frighten her. "It's been two years since I've seen you."

"I'm not very well, Helen," the other replied, wearily. "I've about given up all hope of ever seeing any better days. But what brings you here? I didn't expect ever to see you again."

"Now, Nell, don't talk that way," Helen protested. "You know—or maybe you don't know it—that I would do anything in the world to help you out of this unhappy condition, but Dave's way of looking at things makes it impossible. If you had any vitality I would urge you to leave him and earn your own living."

"But I haven't any left, Helen," said the discouraged woman; "and I don't believe I'll ever recover any. I've rested hope after hope on Dave's assurances of his ability to make a success in life. Really he is a queer genius, and I don't use the word genius entirely with disrespect. In some ways he's clever, very clever, but in other ways he is the most impossible man you ever knew. I believe he is thoroughly honest, but he has no idea of the value of money or what it means to his family. I believe he is by far the strongest leader among the men, but it does neither him nor his family any good. Many a labor leader would make such power and position a source of revenue for himself, but not Dave. Instead, half of his earnings, when he works, are devoted to the labor cause."

"How does he get such a hold on the miners?" Helen inquired.

"By talk, just talk, and really, I must admit he is the cleverest speaker I ever heard. I've seen an audience of a thousand working men and women stand on their tiptoes and cheer him as if they would burst their lungs. I was proud of him on such occasions, but when we got home to our stale bread and soup I could not help wondering if it was not all a dream and I had not just waked up to the reality of things."

"When will he be home?"

"I wish I could tell you," the woman said, helplessly. "He may be here in five minutes and he may not come before 12 or 1 o'clock tonight."

"Right here is where the holiday charity work of the Flamingo Camp Fire begins," she told herself. Then aloud she added:

"I haven't had much to eat since morning, couldn't eat much this noon in my condition of mind, and I'm hungry; what have you in the house for a Sunday evening lunch, Nell?"

"Not much, Helen," was the reply. "Only a half a loaf of rye bread and some corn molasses. The children used to be very fond of that, but they've had it so often since the strike began, that they're almost sick of it."

"Is there any store open near here where I can go and buy something?"

"There's a bakery and delicatessen over on the street where the car line runs. It's probably open now."

"Will I find a drug store over there, too? I want to use the telephone."

"Yes, you'll find a drug store on that street, a block north."

"I'll go at once and you set the table while I'm gone. We'll have a feast that will delight the hearts and stomachs of these little ones."

"God bless you, Helen," were the last words that fell on her ears as she went out.

"I must call up Marion and tell her where I am," she mused as she hastened toward the drug store. "I would have told her where I was going before I left, but I was afraid she wouldn't let me go. Besides, I don't feel like telling her everything yet."

A few minutes later she was in the drug store applying for permission to use the telephone.

"The phone is out of order," the druggist replied.

"Oh," Helen exclaimed in disappointment. "Where is there another in the neighborhood?"

"There is none within half a mile that I know of, except in the saloons," was the reply.

"I can't go there," the girl said desperately. "And I must have a telephone soon. Won't yours be fixed before long?"

"I hope so," said the druggist. "I've sent in a call for a repair man. Can't you come back in an hour or two?"

"Yes, I think so," Helen said, turning to go. "I do hope it is repaired then, because it's very important."

CHAPTER XVII

HELEN DECLARES HERSELF

Twenty minutes later Helen returned to her brother's home, her arms loaded with cured meats, bread, a pie, some frosted cup-cakes, a glass of jam, and a bottle of stuffed olives.

"There," she said, as she deposited her bounteous burden on the table. "I couldn't get any tea or sugar or butter, but even without those we can have quite a feast in a very short jiffy."

"I have some tea and some light brown sugar, which the children like on their bread for a change after they've got tired of corn syrup," Mrs. Nash said.

"Good!" exclaimed Helen with genuine enthusiasm. "That's fine! Butter and white sugar are unnecessary luxuries sometimes. Now we'll get busy and will soon be feasting like a royal family."

And there was no mistake in her prediction. True, it was an extremely democratic royalty—proletariat, to be more exact—but no child prince or princess ever enjoyed the richest viands in a king's dining room more than little Margaret, Ernest and Joseph Nash enjoyed the feast spread before them by the girl auntie they had not seen for two years.

The conversation between Helen and Mrs. Nash, interrupted by the former's errand to the delicatessen and drug stores, was taken up again at the table of the royal feast. The way the children laughed and "um-um-ed" over the "goodies" did Helen's heart good and rendered even cheerful her discussion of a distressing subject.

"What in the world ever brought you here, Helen?" was the question put by Mrs. Nash, after full confidence in the sincerity of Helen's mission, whatever it was, had supplied her with courage to converse with her sister-in-law with perfect frankness. "You didn't come to Hollyhill just to visit us, did you?"

"No, I didn't," Helen answered slowly, "and that fact need not hurt your feelings any, Nell. You'll understand what I mean when I've finished my story. I am attending a girl's school at Westmoreland. We are all Camp Fire Girls, and thirteen of us and a guardian came to Hollyhill on a mission in harmony with Camp Fire teachings, that is, to work among the poor and suffering families of the strikers during the holidays."

"What?" exclaimed Mrs.Nash. "Do you mean to tell me that you are one of the girls visiting at the home of Old Stanlock, the mine owner?"

"Yes, I am," Helen replied, looking curiously at the startled woman.

"Then you mustn't stay here any longer. You must hurry right back. You are in great danger, I tell you, very great danger. The fact of your being my husband's sister won't do you any good. There are some bad men around here, and they're as smart as they are bad. Sometimes I wonder if they are really miners, or if they are not an accomplished bunch of professional crooks."

"What makes you think that?" Helen inquired.

"Well, for one reason, I've been told it. But before anybody uttered such a suspicion in my hearing, I suspected something wrong. You see, while Dave seems to be the leader in the strike, he is in fact only a puppet in the hands of a band of the worst kind of crooks, who are using him to keep the miners in line."

"Who are they?" asked Helen.

"I don't know them all. I know of only half a dozen. They have been here at the house a number of times. The man who seems to dominate them all is a man known as 'Gunpowder' Gerry, a powerful, cunning, sly-eyed fellow about 45 years old. He is the business agent of the union and runs everything, although few persons know it. In some mysterious way he has got a very strong hold on Dave and can make him do anything he wants him to."

"Why do you think I am in danger here?" was Helen's next question.

"Because I've heard some talk here about what would happen if you girls attempted to carry out your plans. They had a spy, a chauffeur, in Mr.Stanlock's home, and he found out all about it. Gerry used this to work up bad blood among the strikers, using Dave as his tool as usual. The threat reached my ears that if you girls came down here in Mining Town, you would never get out alive. They think it is just a move to put something over."

"Did you know that Dave came to Westmoreland a few weeks ago and called at the institute to see me?" Helen asked.

"No, did he? What for? I thought he didn't have any use for you. Excuse me for putting it that way, but it's the way he talks."

"I suppose so. That's because we objected so much to his way of doing. But I found out on that occasion that there really was a tender place in his heart for us. He wanted me to do something to call off our vacation plans, as he was afraid something would happen."

"Why didn't you?"

"Because I didn't take him very seriously. But when on the day before we started for Hollyhill I happened into the postoffice at Westmoreland and caught him in the act of mailing a letter to Marion Stanlock, I became somewhat alarmed. I forced the truth from him after the letter was mailed. He said he was sending her a threatening letter in the hope that it would break up our plans. I asked him why he came to Westmoreland to mail it. He replied that he was afraid it would be traced to him if he mailed it in Hollyhill. Then he urged me, almost commanded me, to prevent our plans from being carried out. He declared that every one of us would probably be killed if we came. I promised to do my best. I watched Marion, hoping to see her read the threatening letter. I saw it after it was laid on her desk in her room. I saw her glance at it and put it into her handbag before she went to bed. Next morning I waked her early and laid the handbag right before her eyes, hoping she would take the letter out and read it. I did not dare to do anything more, but resolved to watch the events closely. Marion read the letter on the train. It was signed with a skull and cross-bones. We decided to give up our original plans, but came on to Hollyhill."

"What did you hope to accomplish by coming to see Dave?" Mrs. Nash inquired.

"I am going to put the matter right square up to him and demand that he lay bare the whole plot that he has been hinting at. If he doesn't, I'm going to tell him that I am going to lay the whole matter before the police."

"You'll probably have to do it. I don't believe he'll ever betray the men who control his gifts and his weaknesses as they would handle a child."

"He really is a child in some respects, isn't he?"

"Absolutely. In fact, I believe he is half sane and half insane, and he is just smooth enough to conceal his insanity from the miners."

"Have you any objection, Nell, to my going after him good and strong?" Helen asked.

"Not in the least. I wish you would, only I'm afraid the results won't be of much advantage to any of us. And I wish you wouldn't stay here late, for I am afraid to have you start back alone after dark."

"I'll make him take me back," Helen said resolutely. "And I want to reassure you in one respect, if you are afraid of consequences to yourself and the children."

"Oh, don't let that bother you," Mrs. Nash interrupted. "You couldn't make conditions much worse than they are now, and you may accidentally make them better."

"But I have something to say that you ought to know," Helen continued. "When father died, it was generally supposed that he left nothing for his family. For years he drew a good salary as a mining superintendent. Well, he didn't leave much, except about $5,000 insurance, but mother had been saving for years secretly, not even letting him know how much she had. He supposed we were living up his salary of $10,000 a year as we went along, for it wasn't in him to save a cent. Mother took a good deal of delight in her secret. For a while she had done her best to induce him to save something, and then, realizing that her plea was futile, she got busy herself in a systematic manner and in the course of seven or eight years she laid aside something like $25,000.

"But shortly before father's death something happened that caused her to guard her secret up to the present time. A large amount of money was stolen from the company that employed father, and mother realized at once that if it were discovered that she had so much money, suspicion might be directed toward him. In fact, she took me into her confidence only about a year ago.

"Now, mother has often said that she would like to do something for you and the children, but Dave's peculiarities always stood in the way. I just wanted to tell you that mother is able and willing to help you and will not let you or her grandchildren suffer as a result of what I may be forced to do."

The conversation went along in this manner for more than an hour. Neither of the sisters-in-law realized how rapidly the time was flying until dusk fell so heavily that it became necessary to light the gas in order to see each other's faces.

"My, what time is it?" Helen questioned, looking at her watch. "Why, it's nearly seven o'clock, and I haven't telephoned to Marion yet. They'll have the whole police force out looking for me if I don't get her on the wire pretty soon. I'll run over and see if that phone is repaired yet. If it isn't I'll have to take a car and ride on to the next drug store; but I'll be back before very long."

"I wish you wouldn't come back tonight, Helen," Mrs. Nash pleaded. "I'm so afraid of those men. Why not go straight to Stanlocks' and send word to Dave that you wish to meet him somewhere tomorrow?"

"I'd rather handle it this way," the girl answered a little stubbornly. "I tell you what I'll do—I'll have them send the chauffeur with the automobile over here after me. That'll be the best way."

With this reassuring announcement, Helen put on her coat and hat and went out. But she would not have proceeded so confidently if she could have caught a glimpse of the figure of a man dashing far up the alley in the rear and have realized that this man had crouched in an eavesdropping attitude for an hour or more at the kitchen door and overheard most of the conversation between her and her sister-in-law.

One, two blocks he ran, then through a gateway and into a house similar to nearly every other house in the street. Two men, a woman, and a child 10 years old looked expectantly toward him as he entered.

"All ready!" cried the latter. "She's coming down the street on this side. Hurry up, Lizzie. Get your coat and hood on. Remember what you are to say: father gone, mother sick. If she won't come in with a little begging, make a big fuss, cry and plead for all you're worth. There you are, all ready. Remember, you get a new coat if you bring her in here."

The speaker opened the door and almost shoved the pale-faced, trembling child out upon her strange mission.

CHAPTER XVIII

HELEN IN THE MOUNTAINS

It was snowing. The flakes that fell were not large fluffy ones; they were small and compact, so that as the northwest wind drove them into Helen's face, she realized that she was being pelted with something more substantial than eiderdown.

The severity of the storm startled the girl. It spurred her to a fuller consciousness of her obligation to her friends, that she remove from their minds all occasion for worry as to her whereabouts as soon as possible.

Putting her muff up to shield her face from the cutting blast, Helen set out bravely up the street. She was not a timid or timorous girl. In fact, the words of warning uttered by her sister-in-law had made no lasting impression on her mind, so far as her own personal safety was concerned. She scarcely thought of looking out for danger from any human agency as she left the house.

As the storm was beating into her face, she did not attempt to look ahead much farther than each step as it was taken. It was necessary for her to lean forward slightly and push her head, as it were, right into the storm, and before she had reached the nearest corner it became evident that she must undergo no little inconvenience, if not actual suffering, before her evening's mission were completed.

"Well, maybe this exercise will give me just the life I need to talk real business to Dave when he comes," she mused, punctuating her conjecture with a gasp or two as she fought against a gust of wind that forced her almost to a standstill. Winning this skirmish with the storm, she pressed forward again, when suddenly another gasp was forced from her by an entirely different cause. She almost stumbled over an object directly in her way, and as she recovered her equilibrium she recognized before her the form of a small girl scantily clad in a short-sleeved coat much too small for her and a hood that came down scarcely far enough to cover her ears. Her hands were bare and she held them up pitifully before the comfortably—to her richly—clad maiden so out of her element in this poverty-stricken district.

"Please, Miss," the girl pleaded; "won't you come and help me? Ma's sick— she fainted—and pa's gone away. I'm all alone with her. Ma's down on the floor an' don't move—I'm afraid she's dead. Oh, please do come, Miss, just a minute, and—"

"Where do you live?" Helen interrupted, indicating by her tone of sympathy that she would do as requested.

"Right there," the little girl replied, pointing with her hand toward one of the houses a short distance ahead. "Come on, please. Just a minute—help me get ma on the bed. I'll find one of the neighbors to help after that."

"All right, go ahead," Helen directed.

"It seems that I am fated to do at least a little of the work that we set out to do, but were prevented from doing by some unfriendly interests. It's a pity some of these people are so prejudiced, for we could really do a lot for them."

Helen's small conductress led the way to the entrance of a miner's cottage that, to all outward appearance from the front, was dark within.

"Haven't you any light?" she asked a little apprehensively, drawing back as if hesitating to enter.

"Oh, yes," the other replied almost eagerly, it seemed. "There's a lamp burning in the kitchen, and I'll light the gas in the front room. Come on, please."

"Where is your mother?"

"She's layin' down on the floor in the kitchen. Come on, I've got a match. I'll light the gas in the front room."

If Helen had obeyed a strong impulse that was tugging within her to hold her back, she would have refused to enter. Perhaps the reason she did not obey that impulse was the fact that a desperate effort to think of another reasonable method of procedure was fruitless and she must either go ahead as she had started or turn away in confusion and leave the little girl in her distress and without an explanation. The latter opened the door and Helen followed her inside.

It was difficult for the visiting Camp Fire girl to figure out any reason why she should be fearful of anything this slip of a child might do, and yet the first act of the latter after they were inside sent through her a chill of terror. Slipping around her like an eel, the little emissary of trouble pushed the door to and turned the key in the lock. Helen was certain also that she heard the key withdrawn from the lock.

Still her conductress, clever little confidence girl that she was, spoke words of reassurance that dispelled some of her victim's fears.

"Wait," she said; "I dropped my match. I'll have to go in the kitchen for another."

Helen's eyes followed the dim form of the child, as the latter moved across the room, and observed for the first time a line of light under what appeared to be a door between the front room and the kitchen. A moment later the door swung open, and she was considerably relieved when she saw lying on the floor the apparently limp and unconscious form of a woman.

Instantly the rescuer's Camp Fire training in the reviving of a person from a faint stimulated in her a sort of professional interest in the task before her, and she started forward to begin work at once. First she must loosen her patient's clothing to make it as easy as possible for her to breathe. Then she must get her in a supine position with her head slightly lower than any other part of her body in order that the brain might get a plentiful supply of blood. The air in the house was heavy and stuffy—the front and rear doors must be thrown open. She must dash cold water upon the face and chest of the patient and rub her limbs toward her body. She ought to have some smelling salts or ammonia, but as these were lacking she must get along without them, unless the daughter of the unconscious woman were able to supply something of the sort.

These things flashed through Helen's well-trained mind as she moved rapidly toward the kitchen. All apprehension of treachery left her as she beheld the evidence corroborating the story of distress that had brought her into the house. Then suddenly the whole apparent situation was transformed into one of the most terrifying character.

A slight noise to her right caused her to turn. Then a piercing scream escaped her lips as she saw a door open and beheld the dim outlines of two burly men approaching her. At the sound of her cry of alarm, they dashed forward like two wild beasts.

The first one seized her around the neck to shut off further alarm. As those muscular fingers closed in upon her throat, it seemed suddenly as if her head were about to burst. Then as the thumping in her ears almost completed the deadening of her auditory nerves, she indistinctly heard these words uttered in a hoarse voice:

"Look out, Bill; don't kill her."

As if surprised back into his senses, "Bill" loosened his hold on Helen's throat. She did not struggle or attempt to cry out again. Evidently the purpose of the ruffians did not contemplate murder, and she realized that there was no wisdom in anything but submission on her part now.

But she was not given time to recover completely before the next move of her captors was made. While one of them held her in a vise-like grip, the other shoved a gag into her mouth and tied the attached strings tightly around the base of her head. Then he bound her hands together in front of her with a strip of cloth.

"There," said the man whom the other had addressed as Bill, "you set down in that chair and keep still and you won't get hurt. But the instant you go to makin' any racket you're liable to breathe your last. All right, Jake, go and get the machine."

"Jake!" The exclamation, though not uttered, was real enough in her mind. Even with the deafening pulse of choking confusion in her head, it had seemed that there was something familiar in the man's voice when he warned "Bill" not to kill her. Was it possible that this was Mr.Stanlock's former automobile driver?

Jake went out the back way, closing the door between the front room and the kitchen as he went. Helen was now left alone in darkness with Bill, who, she thankfully observed, seemed disposed to pay no attention to her so long as she remained quietly in the old loose-jointed rockingchair in which she was seated.

Ten minutes later an automobile drove up in front of the house and Jake reappeared.

"It's almost stopped snowing, luckily," he remarked, "or we'd have our troubles makin' this trip tonight. A little more snow and a little more drifting and we'd be in a pretty pickle."

Helen was certain she recognized Jake's voice now. How she wished she could get a glimpse of his face in even the poorest candle light.

Bill now threw a large shawl over her head and brought it around so that it concealed both the gag over her mouth and the rag manacle on her wrists. Then he pinned it carefully so that it might not slip awry, and ordered her to go with him quietly out to the automobile. Jake had just made an inspection up and down the street and reported the coast clear.

"Now, mind you, young lady," Bill warned significantly; "not a word or a wiggle out o' the ordinary or you'll get your final choke, and you know what that means."

Yes, Helen knew, and she had no intention of futilely provoking a repetition of such punishment. She accompanied her captors submissively and was assisted into the machine. Then something happened which might almost be said to have delighted her if it were not for the strain of benumbing fear that was gripping her.

Jake went around in front of the machine to crank it. For one moment the strong acetylene light from one of the lamps fell full upon his face. Helen recognized it. Her surmise as to his identity was not a mistake.

A minute later the automobile was traveling at a high rate of speed over the streets. Ten minutes later it passed the city limits and was kicking the three inches of snow up along a country highway. On, on it sped, one mile, two miles, on, on, until the probable distance Helen was unable to conjecture, on, on, over smooth roads and rough roads, up hill and down hill, into the mountains. Then suddenly "Bill," who sat in the seat beside her, pulled a light-weight muffler from his pocket and tied it over Helen's eyes, saying coarsely:

"Not that I'm afraid you'll do any mischief with those pretty eyes of yours, but we may as well guard against accidents. You couldn't trace this route again, anyway, could you?"

Helen did not attempt to answer with either a shake or a nod of her head. She was disappointed at the act of her captor in blindfolding her, for she had been watching their course as closely as possible in order to photograph it upon her mind for future reference.

Jake was a good driver—that much must be said for him; and yet, after they struck the mountain road the progress was much slower. From the time when her eyes were bandaged, Helen's only means of determining the character of the road over which they were traveling was the speed or slowness of the automobile. Nor could she compute satisfactorily the time that passed during the rest of the trip.

But it ended at last. The machine stopped, Helen knew not where, and she was assisted out by the two men, who led her, still blindfolded, along a fairly smooth trail, up the side of a mountain or steep hill, then along a fairly level stretch, until at last the prisoner knew that she was passing under a canopy or roof of some sort, for there was no snow under foot. Moreover their footfalls produced a sound, somewhat of the nature of a soft resonant reverberation of a million tiny echoes.

But presently they were out in the open again, as evidenced by the snow and the brisker atmosphere, and Helen shrewdly observed to herself:

"That was a tunnel, I bet anything."

Two hundred feet farther up another gentle incline they reached a place of habitation and entered. Helen had no idea as to the appearance of the exterior, but when the bandage was removed from her eyes, and she was able to look about her, she made a clever surmise, not very far from the truth, that she was in a log cabin.

Every inch of the walls and ceiling, except the windows and doors, was plastered. The doors and windows were fitted in the crudest kind of casing. A few unframed, colored pictures were pasted on the walls. The furniture of the room consisted of a few chairs, a table and an old trunk. A kerosene lamp on the table lighted the room.

"Here's one of them, Mag," said Bill, addressing a large, coarse featured, but remarkably shrewd-eyed woman who opened the door and received them. "Can you keep her safe?"

"You bet your bottom dollar I can keep her safe as long as there is any dough in it for me," was the reply in almost a man's voice.

"Well, get into good practice on this one a-keepin' prisoners," the first speaker advised. "We're goin' to have a dozen more here before long, and then you will have some job."

CHAPTER XIX

THE SUBTERRANEAN AVENUE

For more than half an hour Mr.Stanlock waited upstairs nervously, eagerly, expectantly, apprehensively, for a report from Lieut. Larkin and the four men who remained in the cellar of the Buchholz house to move the pile of scrap lumber, under which it was suspected might be found a clew as to the whereabouts of the missing twelve girls. Interest in the search within the building had suspended other activities in the neighborhood, as it was felt that further progress must depend upon results at this point.

So the score or more of uniformed and citizen policemen waited as patiently as they could in or around the house of mystery, becoming more and more impatient as the minutes grew into the twenties and then the thirties, and still nobody came upstairs to announce indications of success or failure. The noise of the striking pieces of lumber against one another had not been heard for more than twenty minutes. In fact, no sound of any kind came up the cellarway following the first quarter of an hour of rapid labor on the part of the five active searchers below.

At last one of the men, more nervously eager for information than the rest, shouted down the cellarway to the lieutenant, inquiring how he and his helpers were getting on. There was no answer.

He shouted again. Still no reply. Then he announced his intention to descend into the cellar to investigate.

"Wait," said Mr.Stanlock. "There are some tracks in the dust on the steps, and Lieut. Larkin doesn't want them disturbed. Let me go."

Although his apprehensions had not diminished, the mine owner's nerve was considerably strengthened by this time, perhaps as a result of his return from a stuffy basement atmosphere into a region of better ventilation. As he started down the steps with the flashlight of one of the policemen in his hand, he was surprised to feel a strong current of wind blowing upward into his face.

"They must have opened one of the windows," he surmised; but he quickly dismissed the suggestion after flashing his light around the cellar. The pile of lumber had been moved to the opposite side and in the section of the floor it had formerly occupied was a hole three feet in diameter.

"That's where the wind comes from," Mr.Stanlock decided. "It's the mouth of the old mine we used to hear about years ago. But where's the other opening? Funny nobody knows about that. This end has been covered up with that old heavy door and concealed with a layer of earth. When our men moved the pile of lumber, they observed that the earth had been disturbed recently and shoveled it away and found this hole."

Mr.Stanlock directed the rays of light into the hole and discovered a flight of steps cut in the hard clay.

"The lieutenant and his men are down in there," he concluded. "I think I'll follow them."

He descended cautiously into the hole. Half a dozen irregularly formed steps brought him to a slope leading downward on an inclined plane of six or seven degrees. He was astonished at the degree of preservation of the walls, ceiling, and supports, considering the years that had elapsed since the mine was last worked. The passage continued as a downward slope for about fifty yards and then became almost level for a like distance. Only in two places had the walls or ceiling fallen in to any considerable extent, and in neither of those places was the obstruction so great as to constitute an impassable barrier.

As he proceeded, Mr.Stanlock peered ahead anxiously, in the hope that he would discover the lights of Lieutenant Larkin and his companions. But he walked nearly 100 yards through an irregular and characteristically jagged passage before he caught sight of anything indicating that there was anybody besides himself in the abandoned mine. Then suddenly, rounding a sharp point he came upon the advance party of searchers approaching him.

"What did you find?" the mine owner inquired before any surprise greetings could be exchanged. "There's another outlet to this place somewhere, isn't there?"

"Yes, there is," was the reply of the officer in charge. "This gallery runs on for another hundred yards, piercing Holly Hill right through the center. You know the bluff and the rocky slope behind the old mill. Well, it seems that this mine was cut right through at that point, but there was a cave-in that filled up that opening. These rascals that kidnapped the girls evidently were associated with the people that rented the Buchholz place and cut the passage through. The girls have been here all right, but they're gone. They've been taken out of this end of the mine and spirited away in some manner. This means that the scoundrels have a larger and more effective organization than we have ever suspected. Such a case of wholesale kidnapping was never heard of before."

"How can you tell they passed through here?" Mr.Stanlock asked.

"By this principally," the lieutenant answered, holding up a woman's handkerchief that he had picked up; "and by the fact that there is a trail in the snow from the opening of the mine to the alley behind the old mill."

Mr.Stanlock's face shone deathly pale in the glare of the flash lights. The new element of suspense had brought him again to the danger-point of a collapse that had compelled him to withdraw from the active search nearly an hour before.

His voice reflected the distressing strain under which he was laboring as he put his next question:

"What became of them then?"

"That's the problem we've got to solve," Larkin replied. "Apparently they were loaded in automobiles and rushed off to some retreat of the scoundrels."

"How in the world could they do it without somebody's seeing or hearing what was going on?"

"Oh," said the lieutenant without a suggestion of doubt in his voice; "that wasn't very difficult if there were enough of them working together. The evidence of cleverness and skill is not nearly so much in the handling of this affair at the mill end of the mine as at the house end. That was a mighty smooth piece of work, getting all of those girls into that old house, however it was done. Mark my word, you'll find that a very clever trap was set for them. But come on, we've got to get busy before the snow makes it impossible to follow them."

CHAPTER XX

TWELVE GIRLS IN THE MOUNTAINS

Ethel Zimmerman and Ernestine Johnson fainted. All of the rest of the twelve girls who had been decoyed into the Buchholz house by the "sympathetic Mrs. Eddy" were thrown into a panic. And the terror of the situation was not mollified in the least by the sudden appearance on the scene of five men.

Where the men came from so suddenly was not at all clear. Undoubtedly they had been hidden somewhere, but that place could not be determined, for none of the girls remembered from what direction they had made their appearance, north, south, east, west, up, or down. They were just there, and that was all there was to it.

The men did not look like ruffians exactly, although they were not clad in "gentlemen's clothes." The girls were huddled together in the dark scantily-furnished front room, which at some time probably had served the purpose of a combined parlor and reception room. The next apartment, probably designed as a living room, was lighted by a single gas jet turned low.

Ethel and Ernestine fainted in the midst of the address of warning and command from the spokesman of the plotters. This was a signal for a rally to their aid on the part of the other Camp Fire Girls best gifted with presence of mind. Marion led this move, and was quickly assisted by Ruth Hazelton, Julietta Hyde, and Marie Crismore. No objection was offered by the men to this proceeding, as they were intelligent enough to realize that the success of their plot depended largely on a careful guard against a noisy panic that would attract attention from without.

"Somebody get some water quick," Marion directed, as she proceeded to go through the reviving formula in which all of them had been thoroughly drilled.

"I'll get some," "Mrs. Eddy" volunteered, indicating by her offer and actions that she was an efficient ally of the kidnappers. She hastened into the kitchen and soon returned with a large dipper of water. Marion took it from her and sprinkled some of the liquid on the faces of the unconscious girls. The latter quickly recovered and sat up.

But meanwhile the five men were not idle. The leader addressed the girls again with more gentle words and manner, realizing, as only an intelligent criminal may do, that a confidence man's method is the best method for producing a desired illegal effect. In a degree, he was successful, attempting to reassure the captives in the following manner:

"Now, girls, you have nothing to fear from us, if you obey orders. We don't wish to harm a hair on any of your heads. We are merely determined to get what we have set out for, and we are going to use you to help us get it. If you try to balk our purpose, you must take the consequences. Otherwise you will suffer only such inconveniences as go naturally with the experience of being kidnapped. And try to realize this, that being kidnapped isn't such a terrible thing if you are in the custody of gentlemen kidnappers. That's what we are—gentlemen kidnappers. All we ask of you is that you prove yourselves to be what gentlemen kidnappers prefer above all others, namely, real ladylike prisoners.

"Now," he added after a pause during which he surveyed his audience as if to determine the effect of his words; "as soon as the two young ladies who were so unfortunate as to make the mistake of connecting a tragic prospect with this affair have fully recovered, we will proceed."

"That fellow is disguised," declared Marion in a whisper to the girls nearest her. "In fact, all of them are. Observe that every one of them wears a beard, moustache or short side whiskers. Watch their eyes and mouths and every expression on their faces so that we may be able to identify them if we are ever called upon to do so."

"Now, girls," said the spokesman with well simulated gentleness, "no more of that. We don't want to be unduly rude with you, but if there is any more whispering, we'll have to resort to measures that will make it impossible. Now, I think you are all ready, so just follow the leader and some of us will bring up the rear. We will proceed first into the basement."

Tremblingly the twelve Camp Fire Girls followed two of the men down the cellar steps. It was evident to them that resistance would be worse than useless. A single blow from the fist of one of those powerful men would stun any of the girls, if it did not knock her unconscious. In fact their captors could make quick work of them if necessary, and, cooped up as they were in this isolated prison, they could scarcely hope to send forth an effective cry of distress before they were rendered physically incapable of sounding further alarm.

All of the "gentlemen kidnappers" were supplied with electric flash lights, with which they illuminated the cellar and revealed to their captives a hole three feet in diameter in the ground floor and seemingly a flight of steps leading downward.

"Don't get scared, young ladies," advised the "gentlemanly leader" of the "gentleman kidnappers" softly. "That hole is merely the mouth of an old coal mine. We will conduct you through the mine to the other end, which is concealed from public view at a distance, and there we will find four automobiles waiting for you. Lead the way, comrad kidnappers."

The two head men descended into the hole, and the girls followed Indian file. The spokesman and one other man descended last as a rear guard. One of the men remained in the cellar with "Mrs. Eddy" and together they hurriedly replaced the old door over the mouth of the mine, shoveled some loose earth over this and then covered the earth with eight or ten thicknesses of scrap lumber loosely tossed in a heap.

Meanwhile the girls, guided by the lights ahead and aided by the two lights behind, which were directed helpfully along their path, made their way laboriously down the slope and along the many-angled gallery to the opening at the other side of Holly Hill, as the high, rounded elevation on and around which the city was built was called. Under different circumstances undoubtedly they would have been much interested in this experience as a subterranean exploration. And they had all the time they might need for such exploration, for the dusk of evening had not yet developed into darkness and they had to wait in the mine over an hour before it was deemed safe to venture out with the captives.

Near the opening at the foot of the bluff behind the abandoned flour mill, gags were tied tightly over the girls' mouths and their hands were bound in front of them, and they were assisted one by one down a gradual, but rough, incline and into the waiting machines. Snow falling in millions of huge flakes, a fact that evidently caused the kidnappers more worry than the possibility of detection by persons in the vicinity, for remarks escaped some of them relative to the importance of haste before the roads became impassable to automobiles. But the storm served them one good purpose if it menaced them in another respect. It rendered the darkness of the night more impenetrable and kept the streets almost free of pedestrians. Moreover, the plotters were well supplied with means and methods of guarding against escape or rescue. The gags and cloth manacles were so well made that one might have suspected them of being products of a manual training school of burglars' wives. During the passage from the mine to the automobiles each of the girls wore a shawl thrown over her head and pinned close in front, thus concealing both the gags and the manacled condition of their hands.

At last they were all in the machines, each of which was in charge of a driver. Three of the girls were put into each automobile and one of the men got in with them to see that their conduct was as per scheduled program. Then the start was made.

On, on they went, out into the country and along a road that Marion knew led into the heart of the mountains. She could see the dim, shadowy form of High Peak in the distance. Meanwhile, as she peered out eagerly into the darkness with an irrational longing for rescue from some miraculous source—for this was the only kind of rescue that seemed possible under the circumstances—she kept working at the bonds about her wrists and the gag in her mouth slyly and without obvious effort, until with joy she realized that she was at least partly successful.

"I am certain I could shove that thing right out of my mouth and give the most piercing scream ever heard if somebody would only come along and hear me," she told herself.

The snow kept on falling heavily, much to the alarm of the kidnappers and the joy of the kidnapped, but the automobiles reached the mountains before there was any serious delay. It looked indeed as if the trip would be successful from the point of view of the captors of the Camp Fire Girls. But at last the snow became so deep that the girls could feel that the automobiles were laboring under almost insurmountable difficulties. Marion heard several curses uttered by the chauffeur, and the man inside the car echoed them once or twice. Finally the automobile came to a full stop and the driver could force it along no further. A consultation, with all three of the men taking part, was held.

In the midst of their debate, something happened that changed the aspect of things almost as completely as might have been accomplished if Marion's dream of a miraculous rescue had been realized. Other persons were on the scene and they were talking to the driver, inquiring if they could be of any assistance.

"We're a patrol of Boy Scouts," one of the new arrivals said. "We've lost our way, but that doesn't need hinder our helping you out of your scrape. Maybe you can direct us how to find our way back."

Marion never felt a more intense thrill in her life than she felt at the sound of that voice. She looked out of the window and saw a group of eight or ten boys, each of them carrying a gun, close to the automobile.

With an effort that had behind it all of the power of the most joyous impulse of her life, she swung her bound clinched fists right through the pane of glass, pushed the gag from her mouth, and shouted:

"Clifford! Clifford! This is Marion. All of us girls are being kidnapped by these men. Shoot these rascals and shoot to kill."

CHAPTER XXI

THIRTEEN GIRLS IN THE MOUNTAINS

Marion's plea for aid did not reach Clifford and the other Boy Scouts to whom it was addressed without interruption. The latter half of it came in jerked and disjointed phrases, and the tone of utterance was one of extreme fear and distress. Clifford and Ernie Hunter, the leader of the patrol, although amazed beyond description, realized that this appeal for assistance was no idle one, and it was up to them to do something quickly or action on their part might soon be too late.

"You boys take care of the men in front, and Clif and I will settle this affair back here," Ernie shouted. "Don't let them escape."

With these words, the patrol leader seized the latch of the nearest auto door and pressed down on it. As he did this, the door flew open with a heavy swing, and Ernie jumped aside just in time to ward off a body-lunge blow from the fist of a man who sprang out of the machine like a beast leaping with all fours.

In less time than it takes to tell it, two of the men had broken through the cordon of Boy Scouts around the automobile and disappeared in the darkness. The third, Mr.Stanlock's chauffeur, was not so desperately courageous. The menace of two or three gun muzzles held within a few feet of his face was more than he cared to oppose, so he remained a prisoner.

"Look out, boys," called out Hazel Edwards. "There are three more automobiles coming along behind with desperate men in them. Each of those autos has three girl prisoners in charge of two men, one of them the driver."

"Miles, you and Hal and Jerry stay here and guard the prisoner and protect the girls against those rascals if they return," Ernie directed. "The rest of us will run back a short distance and meet the next machine before they suspect something wrong."

As he finished speaking, Ernie led the way, followed by four other boys, back through the snow twenty or thirty yards, and then stopped and listened. A short distance further, they heard a sound the cause of which could not be mistaken. It was the rapid, pulsating chug-chug of an automobile engine. They waited a few minutes, but it appeared to be coming no nearer.

"The snow has stopped this one, too," said Clifford. "Come on and we'll give them a surprise."

A few paces farther brought the boys in view of a machine with the engine running idle and no driver visible in front. Naturally this made them suspicious and a halt was called for a little circumspection. Then, carefully, cautiously, they advanced toward the automobile, keeping nervous watch on all sides to avoid a surprise.

They reached the machine, which they had been able to locate by the noise of the engine, and found it also deserted, save for the three prisoners, bound and gagged, in the car. While the other four in the party of rescuers kept watch against a surprise, Clifford cut the bonds on the wrists of the girls and removed the gags from their mouths.

"Where did the villains in charge of this car go?" was the first question he put to the released prisoners.

"They skipped," replied Violet Munday. "Two men who had been in the machine ahead came back and said the game was up, that they were discovered by a force of Boy Scouts armed with guns and they couldn't afford to put up a fight, for even if they won, the whole country would be aroused and they couldn't hope to carry out their original plans. They went back to warn the other men. No doubt you'll find the other machines abandoned, too."

"All right," said Ernie; "you girls stay here in the car and keep warm. We'll be back as soon as we can find the others."

The boys found the other two automobiles also abandoned and released six more Camp Fire prisoners.

"Now let's return and get the head auto started back first," Ernie proposed.

This plan was adopted. Arrived at the machine in which Marion, Hazel and Julietta had been prison-passengers, they found a new and important development in affairs. Jake, the chauffeur, had confessed. He had offered to conduct the boys to Helen's place of detention and effect her release if the boys would let him go. It was less than half a mile away. The boys agreed. Clifford suggested that the girls remain in the automobile while the Scouts made the proposed raid, but they objected strenuously.

In a short time the rest of the girls were brought forward, informed of the plan, and the start was made. All of the girls insisted on taking part in the expedition. In less than half an hour they were at the door of Helen's prison, where Jake gave the "open sesame" knock.

An uncouth woman opened the door. Behind her stood a man, who proved to be her husband. Jake pushed the astonished pair aside, and went directly to the side of the room opposite the entrance and lifted a bar across a door opening into another department. As he opened this door, Marion rushed forward and was first to greet a slender, pale-faced girl, who stepped out eagerly toward her rescuers.

"Helen!" cried the girls in a chorus.

Jake slipped out and was seen no more.

CHAPTER XXII

A SLEIGHRIDE HOME

That was a meeting not soon to be forgotten. It was a signal for the casting away of every element of secrecy, and Helen told her story.

She told the story of her brother, of his sickness when a child, of the resultant distortion of his character into that of a man of strange and incongruous genius and weakness, and of the embarrassment he had caused her and her mother. He, it was, she said, who had written the skull-and-cross-bones letter.

"Who wrote the other anonymous letter that you received at the Institute?" Hazel Edwards inquired.

"I don't know," Helen replied with a faint smile. "Perhaps these boys can answer that question."

"I must plead guilty to that," announced Clifford, advancing with a bow.

"But what's the surprise you were going to spring?" inquired Ruth Hazelton, mischievously. "Is this it?"

"Now, never you mind," said Clifford. "Things didn't go just right. This kidnapping affair interfered with our plans, and they are hereby called off. We didn't want you to know we were here."

Two of the boys had been dispatched as messengers to Hollyhill for vehicles to take the girls back to Marion's home. About 2 o'clock in the morning Mr.Stanlock, several of his neighbors, and three policemen, led by the two Scout messengers, burst into the room and announced that they had brought three bob-sleds to give them all a sleighride.

And a glorious sleighride home it was for all except the two prisoners, whom the police took into custody.

The story of the CAMP FIRE GIRLS IN THE MOUNTAINS is told, all but the subtitle, "A Christmas Success Against Odds." There was a real success in store for them. The police made a raid, but found that the criminal element that had gained a throttle hold on the labor organization in the mines had cleared out so clean that not a living vestige of them could be discovered. The way was now clear, and the Camp Fire Girls carried out their original plans, successfully and much to the benefit of the poverty stricken families of the strikers.

But the history of Flamingo Camp Fire is by no means complete with this narrative. It seemed to be a peculiar lot of these girls to become associated or in touch with events of novel, interesting, and sometimes thrilling character, and those who would follow their further experiences along these lines should read the second volume of this series, entitled:

CAMP FIRE GIRLS IN THE COUNTRY;orThe Secret Aunt Hannah Forgot.